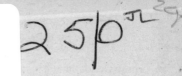

D1337749

Praise for
JOHN D. MACDONALD

"The Dickens of mid-century America—popular, prolific and...conscience-ridden about his environment...a thoroughly American author."
The Boston Globe

"It will be for his crisply written, smoothly plotted mysteries that MacDonald will be remembered."
USA Today

"In McGee mysteries and other novels as well, MacDonald's voice was one of a social historian."
Los Angeles Times

"MacDonald had the marvelous ability to create attention-getting characters who doubled as social critics. In MacDonald novels, it is the rule rather than the exception to find, in the midst of violence and mayhem, a sentence, a paragraph, or several pages of rumination on love, morality, religion, architecture, politics, business, the general state of the world or of Florida."
Sarasota Herald-Tribune

Fawcett Books
by John D. MacDonald

The Damned

JOHN D. MacDONALD

FAWCETT GOLD MEDAL • NEW YORK

A Fawcett Gold Medal Book
Published by Ballantine Books
Copyright © 1952 by John D. MacDonald

ISBN 0-449-12887-3

Manufactured in the United States of America

First Fawcett Gold Medal Edition: June 1952
First Ballantine Books Edition: July 1985
Twenty-first Printing: December 1989

THE DAMNED

Prologue

THE AIR had a clean, new, morning smell. Manuel
Forno paused for a moment on top of the ridge near his
adobe home, to inhale more deeply, to enjoy the morning more thoroughly.

It was, indeed, one of the very best mornings. A good
morning for Manuel Forno, public servant. Off to the
right were the distant cream and white and yellow buildings of San Fernando, village of his birth. And down the
long slope to the left he could see the muddy ribbon of
the Río Conchos, pleasantly gilded by the early sun.

Manuel began to trudge down the slope, humming
snatches of Augustín Lara's bullfight music, "Silverio."
Ai, it would be good to save much money and one day go
to the capital, to the Plaza México, perhaps to see Silverio
Pérez himself.

If one were very careful . . . He shrugged. There
would never be enough pesos. Face it, Manuel. They pay
you a tiny quantity of pesos for pulling hard on a wire
cable. This effort causes a ferry to swim across the Río
Conchos. Free ferry, courtesy of the Estados Unidos de
México. And once the far shore is reached, why, you turn
around and cause the beast of a ferryboat to swim back
again, carrying, at the most, two cars or one large truck
on each voyage.

Face it, Manuel, he told himself. Should you ever save enough pesos, Rosalita will use them to take a *camión* that will carry her, in three hours, north to the bridge between Matamoros and Brownsville, Texas, and there she will arrange to cross the bridge and spend those pesos on *americano* merchandise of fabulous prices.

He sighed heavily, feeling almost sorry for himself. Back and forth across the river all day. A burro, serving the arrogant *turistas*.

And then, as he turned left down the shoulder of the road toward the ferry landing, he cheered up as he remembered the sparkling new ferry that had been provided just recently so that *el presidente* could ride across the Río Conchos in style.

How splendid to be at last rid of that ancient ferry, that grotesque waddling old lady of a ferry, that hideous gray scabbed old beast! The new ferry had paint that would shine in the sun.

And a larger crew. Four men on the catwalk. Manuel felt the sun on his shoulders and knew that it would be a hot day. On such a hot day one should not work too hard. It was bad for the health. Through long practice he had learned that it is possible to appear to be pulling on the pinch bar that grasps the cable without, in reality, using any force at all. It was merely necessary to keep the arms rigid so that the muscles of the back would not appear to be slack. It would be a useful trick on such a day as this.

The road turned and slanted down a steep place in the river bank and he saw the clean shine of new paint. It could make a man proud, rather than ashamed, to cause such a splendid creature to swim back and forth across the river. It was fitting that the Río Conchos should have a new ferry. Once one considered it carefully, it became obvious that this was a most important crossing of a most important river. There was but this one way to go, by vehicle, from the city of Victoria to Brownsville, Texas. Merely this one road, unless, of course, one wished to return to Victoria, drive an incredible distance north to Laredo, Texas, and then travel through Texas east to Brownsville.

He glanced across the river and stopped suddenly, appalled. Cars were lined up on the far side of the river. What a grotesque start for the day, just when one expected a few pleasant hours of leisure, without too many interruptions for the purpose of hauling the craft across the river!

When he came around the bend, he saw that the ferry was not on the near shore. It was, for some reason, about fifteen feet from the shore. And his fellow workers stood hip-deep in the muddy water in front of the ferry, grubbing with shovels.

He stopped again, and a small interior voice advised him that this might be an excellent day to disappear.

But Vascos turned and saw him. "Come here, Manuel Forno!" he bellowed.

Manuel adjusted his face into an expression of amiable idiocy and marched down to stop in front of his diminutive boss, the *jefe* of the ferry, the one who labored only with the tongue.

"What, Vascos, are they doing?"

"Those curious implements are shovels. Perhaps you have heard of them. A shovel is a utensil with which one digs. And there is one for you. Kindly dig."

Manuel stared blankly at him. "Why?"

Vascos' face darkened ominously. "Because you are told to dig, señor. I shall explain. I shall use the little words. Kindly note the river. What do you see?"

"It is smaller than yesterday, Vascos."

"Much smaller, and growing smaller each moment. Perhaps it will disappear entirely. Perhaps you will disappear entirely. Poof! That is too much to hope for."

Manuel eyed the shovel and backed tentatively away. "I shall be glad . . ."

"Come back here. The river has dropped so that it is no longer possible to bring the ferry close enough to shore to either load or unload the vehicles. Thus it becomes necessary to dig with the shovels to create a channel to get the ferry close enough so that large timbers can be used as a ramp rather than the steel one on the ferry. Have I confused you?"

"But the old ferry..." Manuel said weakly.

"The old ferry did not need so much river. We have a new ferry. It is, perhaps, too big for the Río Conchos. On each trip it is necessary to dig with the shovels."

"I do not feel well, Vascos."

"Either use the shovel or it shall be used against your head."

"Vascos, listen to me. I do not have your intelligence. That is certain. However, could we not wait until the river ceases to drop? Then it would only be necessary to dig one time at each bank. Most of those who wait are only tourists. They have no place to go, and they travel with great speed. Let them wait."

Vascos stuck out his chest. "It is my position to keep the ferry in service."

"Such an attitude can be overdone, Vascos."

"Perhaps. But it has been said that Atahualpa will cross sometime today." Vascos took out his handkerchief and wiped his forehead. The mention of the name made the shovels fly faster in the hands of Manuel's fellow workers.

"Ah," said Manuel, "the politico. When that time comes, strength will come to you, Vascos, out of fear. And you shall pick up the ferry on your back and run lightly across the river."

Vascos stared at Manuel for a moment. Then Vascos went over, picked up the shovel, brought it back, and handed it to Manuel with a bow, saying, "If you would be so kind, señor..."

"I wish it were possible for me to say that this is a pleasure," Manuel replied. He went slowly over to the small shack that served as Vascos' office and began, with the slowest motions, to take off his clean white shirt. The men in the river yelled angrily at Manuel, telling him to hurry. Manuel rewarded them with a sad, tired smile. This splendid day had soured itself with startling speed. Three vehicles on this side and many on the other side. He picked up the shovel, examined it inch by inch, and set it down again. He removed his sandals and placed them near the neatly folded shirt.

He picked up the shovel again and walked slowly into

the warm muddy water. The mud spread up through his toes. The others made room for him, gladly.

"This," said Manuel, as he made the first thrust with the shovel, "might become a long and discouraging day."

He began to dig, doggedly, all chance of escape gone. Perspiration oiled his brown shoulders.

I, he told himself, am a picturesque *mexicano*, and the *turistas* with their bright empty faces will be clicking their little black boxes at me as I swing this *hijo* of a shovel.

When work is inescapable, one must perform it. From work comes pesos. From pesos comes food. With food you are able to work. It is a trap. But food keeps Rosalita warm and round, and gives one the necessary strength to do what is necessary and proper to that warm, round brownness. The bait in the trap, perhaps.

He labored, but made certain that he kept an ample amount of energy in reserve. When Atahualpa crossed the river, it would be necessary to work like a madman, beating the brown water to a creamy froth. He debated the results that would come from greeting Atahualpa with a shovelful of mud. No doubt, in three days, the body of one Manuel Forno would rise to the top of the river.

Each time he straightened up, Vascos was watching him. Manuel experimented until he found that precise working speed which would keep Vascos annoyed, yet not give him cause to bellow.

He spewed ahead once more at the vanishing road.
A crazy, pointless thing to do. But done now. Unforeseeable, unforseen. A small, small gate, this one there.

Chapter One

THE ICE-BLUE Cadillac with Texas plates boomed
across the wasteland. Darby Garon held it at ninety, brown
hands lightly on the wheel. Enchiladas and beer in Victoria had been a mistake at midday. The meal was a
sodden, unmoving weight in his stomach. Both side vents
were turned to slam the superheated air in against him
and the girl who sat beside him, her eyes closed. The girl
had been the same sort of mistake as the meal; the difference existed only in degree. She too was highly spiced,
completely indigestible.

Two hundred miles from Victoria to Matamoros. Then
across the bridge into Brownsville, and then a straight
hard run up to San Antone, where he could get rid of her.
Three weeks that had been a crazy, expensive mistake.
He couldn't wait to see the last of her. Betty Mooney was
something he wanted to forget quickly, and knew he
never would. He knew that in some less than obscure way
he had soiled and shamed himself.

The hard high sun sent chrome needles through the
dark lenses of the sunglasses he wore. His cotton short-
sleeved shirt, worn outside khaki walking shorts, was
completely unbuttoned. The wind dried the sweat on his
chest to salt crystals, but each time he leaned back in the
seat, the back of the shirt was soaked through.

Ahead the road disappeared into a dark pool of heat
waves. Wild horses wheeled through the roadside scrub.
Buzzards drew their doom circles against a glaring sky
far off to the left. He felt the sweat track down the
backs of his naked calves. Hell would be a place where you
drove forever under an unmoving sun, riding next to a
big girl in a yellow dress, a girl with her eyes shut.

Darby glanced over at her. The skirt of the yellow dress
was bunched high, and her heavy thighs were slackly
spread. Having eaten, the animal slept.

He scowled ahead once more at the onrushing road. A crazy, pointless thing to do. But done, now. Unforgettably done. At forty-four a man should have more sense. A successful man, with two kids in college, with a trim-bodied charming wife, with a good position with an oil company, with a fine home in Houston. Now the entire structure was rocked. Maybe it had already collapsed. Job and home and wife and kids.

Perhaps this sort of thing had been building for years. That aimless restlessness. The sudden, anticipatory shiver in his guts when he had looked at the young girls in their light dresses.

Having that damnable credit card had made it so much easier. Too easy. He had driven over to San Antonio to straighten out a mix-up on land leases. Routine trip. One of scores that he had made. Fixed it in two days, and then, in the bluing dusk of a long July day, had felt that familiar reluctance to head back toward Houston, toward routine, toward the well-ordered life where a change of breakfast eggs was a major incident.

And he had walked in the dusk streets, and, with the half-apologetic air of a tongue-lolling dog, had followed a tall, ripe-bodied young girl who strolled slowly. Caught up with her at a crossing. Took off his hat to wipe his forehead with his handkerchief, saying, "Warm, isn't it?"

He would never forget her slow bold stare of appraisal, the faint slant of light across her heavy features, as he stood there pleading dumbly for adventure, half frightened at his own temerity, wondering how and where he had lost that casual confidence of his youth that, in years gone by, had made such an approach ridiculously easy. She gave him a long time to wonder what she thought of his long, hard-boned face, the eyes set deep, the jaw elongated, the mouth hinting grimly of New England.

"Hot, I'd call it." Her voice had an odd quality, and it made Darby think of the way his youngest son had sounded during those months just before his voice changed.

"An evening for tall cold drinks in air-conditioned surroundings," he said, feeling the shame of anyone who begs.

"I was going to a movie."

"Alone?"

"Look, I'm no pickup, mister."

"Anyone can see that. I'm a stranger in town. I just thought . . ."

"You mean you were dreaming."

"I'm sorry, miss."

"Well, you've apologized. If you had a car, a ride would be O.K. Just to cool off."

"My car is in a lot three blocks back."

And she walked back with him. She said she was Betty Mooney and she worked in a telephone office. He said he was Darby Garon and worked for an oil company. She walked tall beside him. Her hair was long, heavy, blonde-red. Her features had a funny harshness, a hawkishness. As she walked beside him, he gave sidelong glances at her high, heavy, wide-spaced breasts, at the rolling pelvic tilt of her walk. Her scent was thick in the unstirring air, and she made him feel weak, almost sick, with desire for her.

Her manner changed subtly, became less casual, more holiday-like when he unlocked the door of the long blue car for her. She saw his suitcase on the back seat.

"Going someplace, Darby?"

"Well, I'd checked out and half planned to start back to Houston." His unmeaning laugh was nervous, almost a giggle.

He drove southeast down 181, the Corpus Christi high-way. She sat close to him.

"How old are you, Betty?"

"Twenty-three. You're about thirty-five, aren't you?"

"About."

Old goat, he thought, rolling in the scent of girl flesh. His hands were wet. Moira was the woman who should be riding beside him. Moira never sat that close. Moira's perfume always made him think of the crisp astringency of peppermint. The scent Betty Mooney wore so liberally made him think, crazily, of a rumpled bed.

She hummed a tune, sang the final words. "Let's get away from it all."

"I wouldn't have thought you'd know that one."

"Is it old or something? Coop plays it a lot. He's my favorite disc jock. You listen to him, don't you?"

"No. But I like the sentiment behind that song. Let's get away from it all. What do you think, Betty? Should we get away from it all?"

"Like where?"

"Oh, Mexico City. We'll take a vacation. Like the sound of that?"

"It sounds swell. But I couldn't. You know that."

"And I couldn't take you there. It was just a game."

"You might have got yourself in a sling if I'd said yes, then."

"If you'd said yes, I might have gone through with it." And he knew, surprisingly, that he meant it. Job and family had shrunk. They were sets in a miniature theatre, seen from far away. Reality was Betty Mooney. The rest of it was a clever illusion.

"Down the road on the left there's a place. See it? Sandy's. The liquor isn't legal, but it won't poison you and it's air-conditioned."

They went in. Glass and chrome and soft lights. They knew Betty. The drinks came in coffee cups. He saw her clearly across the booth table, saw her for the first time. He knew from her face and her body that she would not last. At twenty-three she was precariously overripe. In another year or two the firm body would spread and soften, the heavy features begin to sag. At the moment the physical impact of her was as real as a fist blow against his mouth. His hands trembled.

He saw the drinks working on her, and felt them working on him.

"How about that fling?" she said.

"You mean it?"

"If it isn't a budget trip. If it lasts a little while. I don't like my job. And there are lots of jobs nowadays. I've been thinking of a job in a plant. Aircraft. They make real money."

He remembered the credit card. "It won't be a budget trip."

"How about your job?"

"I come and go as I please," he lied.

"Big shot."

"Not really. Just almost. And my wife has long since given up wondering or caring where I am." Forgive me, Moira.

"I know some kids who went down. It's no job getting the permit. I get a card and walk across the bridge. You get one for yourself and the car and drive across and pick me up."

He saw the hard flicker of excitement under her casual air. Tomorrow you can be dead. Hillary popped off last year. Heart. And only forty-six.

There was a moment in San Antonio when he sat in the car on a back street and waited for her to come down with her suitcase. He started the motor, ready to drive away, ready to drive headlong back to sanity. He bit hard on his lip. He saw her coming down the walk toward the car, tall and bountiful, full of all her slow promises.

They stayed what was left of the night at an air-conditioned court near Alice, signed in as Mr. and Mrs. Roger Robinson.

The blindness started there, in her heavy arms. She laughed softly at his eagerness. With the driving, unthinking blindness, with his insatiable need for her, the days went by and the miles went by, and the Hotel del Prado in Mexico City was merely the annex to a tourist court near Alice, Texas. He used her with deadly persistency, and the times in between were merely a nothingness, a waiting. While he napped, she bought clothes in the Mexico City shops.

And then, one morning, he awoke and it was as though he had walked out of a movie, stood blinking on the sidewalk, trying to remember which way to go.

He looked at himself and he looked at her. He had tried to call it a deathless romance, a great love. And the rationalization had shattered suddenly, leaving him naked. He saw a gaunt foolish man of middle years spending his savings on a raw, big-bodied young girl with a limited IQ. The pores of her cheeks and nose were unpleasantly enlarged. In conversation she repeated herself interminably, expressing childish infatuations with movie actors, TV stars, disc jockeys. Her love-making was an unimaginative compound of all the movies she had seen, all the confession stories she had read. He stared in wonder at the meaty mass of her hips, at the lactic, bovine breasts, startled that he should have thought this worth the risk of destroying his world. He realized sourly that he could anticipate her every word, every sigh, every movement. And there was no longer excitement in the sight of her padding, heavy and naked, through the hotel suite. Merely an irritation that she did not cover herself up. The notes to Moira and to the company, notes that had seemed so clever at the moment, with their hints about some secret deal on a Mexican oil concession, now appeared, in retrospect, to be absurd, transparent.

He wanted, near him, the clean astringency that reminded him of peppermint.

And it had ended, that morning. In Mexico City. He had tried to put her on a plane. But even though she had immediately sensed his withdrawal, his distaste, she refused to fly back.

Once, during a long-gone New Hampshire summer, he had been on his uncle's farm. Ginger, a raw-boned setter pup, had killed a chicken. Darby's uncle had tied the limp chicken around Ginger's neck. Darby Garon remembered his pity for the dog, the evident misery and self-disgust in Ginger's eyes.

The cheap little romance had died on a cool sunny morning, but she was still tied to him. They had driven down out of the Sierra Madres into the baked plains. In an incredibly short time they had arrived at that smoldering bitterness which usually takes years of loveless marriage to produce.

During their long silences he thought about himself and what he had done to his life. For twenty years of marriage he had been physically faithful. Twenty years to balance against three weeks of debauchery. Moira would know. It was not fear that shook him. It was the sense of loss, of having discarded something precious.

He glanced at Betty Mooney again. Her yellow dress was dark-stained at waist and armpits. Ahead a ridge of rock slanted close to the shoulder of the road. His shoulder muscles tightened. One hard wrench at the wheel. The day would explode into nothingness and the eye in his mind saw it from the high lens of the cruel buzzard. Blue car crushed and smoking, and the yellow dress a vivid blotch against rock. The rock ridge rushed by and his shoulder muscles slackened again. It was something he could not do. It was too cheap a way to pay for it. The hard puritan streak within him demanded a more difficult expiation of this sin.

The road dipped suddenly and he saw the long line of cars and trucks, frighteningly close, unmoving. The girl slammed hard against the dash as he thrust his foot against the brakes. The car swerved, tires screaming, and he fought the skid. He brought the car at last to a halt about a foot from the rear bumper of the car ahead.

He received angry looks, heard laughter.

"You all right?" he asked Betty. His hands were shaking with reaction, knees trembling.

"Hurt my fingers," she said dully. "You didn't have to be going so damn fast, did you?"

He didn't answer. He got out and looked down the long line. At the foot of the shallow slope he could see a muddy river not more than eighty feet wide. The road was cut down through a high river bank. He could see where it curved up the opposite shore, see the cream and white buildings of a town beyond the opposite bank. It had that cemetery look of all small Mexican towns that drowse through midday heat.

He reached in and took his road map out, unfolded it.

"That's San Fernando over there. And this is the ferry across the Río Conchos. We're still eighty-five miles or so from Matamoros. It looks like something might be wrong with the ferry."

"You don't say," she said acidly.

"I'll walk down and see if I can find out what's the trouble."

"You do that."

He counted the cars and trucks as he went down the slant of the road. They were empty for the most part. There were two small stores set back from the road on the right side, some dusty trees that gave meager shade. He was number twenty-two in line. And traffic was extremely light on the highway. He had seen two cars in the last hundred miles. American tourists, Mexican travelers.

The lead car was a little green MG with Louisiana plates. A young man with a bronze tan, golden hair, and a red silk shirt sat cross-legged on a leather pillow in the shade cast by the little green car.

"How long have you been here?" Darby Garon asked bluntly.

The boy looked him over. He lifted a cigarette to his lips with a dainty grace that was as illuminating as an entire case record in Kraft-Ebbing.

"Since ten-thirty this morning," he said in a girlish voice.

Darby stared at him. "That's . . . better than four hours."

"Really, it seems more like four years. The boy I'm with is just terribly discouraged, believe me. You see, Alemán visited here recently and these dolts bought a new ferry to impress the *presidente*. The thing is too huge for the river and right now the level is dropping and every time they make a trip a lot of little men pounce into the water and scoop out the goo with shovels so they can get close enough to set planks from the shore to the ferry so people can drive up."

Darby thanked him and walked slowly back to the car. He remembered having checked the mileage from Victoria to Laredo. Three hundrd and twenty-one miles. Add another hundred plus back to Victoria. Say four hundred and thirty miles. It might be better than waiting in the heat. And then he remembered the gas. The tank had been three-quarters full when he left Victoria. A shade less than three-quarters. He had been looking for a gas station on the road, hadn't seen one, had planned on getting gas in San Fernando.

Betty was standing beside the car. She raised her eyebrows in question.

"The lead car has been here over four hours. Trouble with the ferry."

"We have to wait?"

"It looks like it."

"I got to have a drink of something cold. See if you can find some beer in one of those stores, sweets. I'm dry as a bone."

"If I can find anything, I'll bring it over to those trees. See if you can find some shade."

He walked slowly toward the nearer of the two grimy little stores. The stores were adobe, and smeared with the inevitable Coca-Cola and Nescafé signs that dapple Mexico like paint stippled from a vast, careless brush. Straw sombreros and serapes, *turista* women in slacks and sun tops, the ragged polite children of the Mexican poor, the rude, screaming brats of the Mexican rich and of the *americanos*. Beer and deep slow laughter of Texans. Sun and dust and an odd flavor to the atmosphere. Darby Garon could sense it clearly. A faint edge of good humor that any minor disaster creates. Plus something moving beneath and behind the good humor. Something ancient and evil. In Mexico the sunshine can have a look of death, he thought.

He moved, stiff-shouldered, through the crowd, and a faint chill seemed to brush the nape of his neck. There was tepid beer packed around a chunk of grainy ice in a lift-top chest. The beer was being sold before it could be chilled. The fat little proprietor was charging three pesos, fifty centavos a bottle. He seemed both frightened and chagrined by his own avarice and boldness.

THE DAMNED

Berry was standing beside the car. She raised her eyebrows in question.

Chapter Two

WHEN the blue Cadillac came to a smoking stop, John
Carter Gerrold took his gaze for just a moment from the
face of his lovely bride and glanced at the car sixty feet
away. John Carter Gerrold and Linda sat on a car robe
spread on the dusty grass in the shade of one of the meager trees that topped the banks of the cut that led down to
the ferry.

They had honeymooned in Taxco, walked the cobble-
stone streets by moonlight, hand in hand, slept in each
other's arms.

There was magic about her. Magic that took his breath.
The moment he had first seen her, he had known that he
would either marry her or be haunted by loveliness unat-
tainable the rest of his life.

Now he looked at her and she seemed a stranger, with-
drawn and enchanted, and it was incredible to him that
in the long quiet nights she had been in his arms, with
the long silk of flank, the warmth, the singing of her body.
Always, in retrospect, the inward vision of the tumbling
violence, the memory of sweet orgy, brought back to him
a curiously objective image of his own greedy use of her,
with galloping heart and thundering breath during the
entwined delving for an utmost togetherness, and in retrospect he felt oddly shamed, as though there was an inde-
cency about it all, and improperness. It brought to
his mind a childhood memory of a day when, hidden in
the bushes, he had seen a swart visitor to his uncle's es-
tate laugh coarsely and strike a kitchen match across the
pure, perfect white marble belly of the garden statue of
the goddess Diana. After they had gone, John had got a
coarse brush and soap from the cook and had scrubbed
away the yellow streak the match had left. It had made a
queer stirring within him to touch the statue. And later,
on a summer night when he had been visiting his uncle,

he crept down to the garden. She had been white and
alive in the moonlight, the weathered coldness of breast
smooth against his cheek, his hands atremble against the
marble loins, and there, in the dewy night, with the crazy
thickening, and then ignoring the cold eyes of God staring down the slant of moonlight, and forgetting the white
milk eyes of the carven Diana, the secret and shameful act,
the thing like a heat and a sickness, with the statue seem-
ing to tilt as though it would fall, and he cried with his
teeth against the grass, wishing it would fall and smash
him utterly.

He looked at his warm goddess beside him now, saw
the utter smoothness of white hair falling thick and
sleek—not precisely white, but with a faint glistening
creaminess. Her brows were black and her face was oval,
the brandied eyes spaced gravely, the lips wide and warm
with instinctive wisdom, the throat and shoulders golden
and fragile above the strapless nubby material of the pale
tan linen dress. She half lay on her side, braced on her
elbow, both knees drawn up, the skirt fanned over them.

John Carter Gerrold did not like her in that position.
It made more pronounced the mound of her hip, and the
front of her dress fell away just enough so that he, sitting
with arms locked around his knees, could see the upper
hemispheres of the smallish breasts that he knew to be
firm, yet not so firm as cool marble, remembered.

Her position seemed to make her fleshier, more woman-
ly. He thought of her often as standing, virginal, in bil-
lowing whiteness, her face lifted to a shaft of light that
came down from an operatic sky.

Had he never touched her then, she would have remained as in the beginning: remote, and with that slow
and lovely enchantment that made all persons soften their
voices when they spoke to her.

He glanced at the thermos. "More water, darling?"

"It's over an hour since they took that last car across.
I think we better ration it."

"Of course. Miserable place, isn't it?"

She turned her head slowly to look up and down the
road. "I like it. I don't know why. I was beginning to

think we were . . . going back too fast. This is a little time to think. And maybe we can talk, John."

He gave her a startled look. She traced the car-robe pattern with her finger. Her hair swung forward, partly masking her face. "Talk! We've talked about everything under the sun."

"All the little things. None of the big things."

"I worship you, Linda. Is that a little thing?"

She tossed her head with a motion that swung the glossy hair back. "I wonder if maybe I just want to be loved. Not worshiped. You . . . you sort of put me in a frame, darling. Or on a pedestal or something."

"Where you belong."

She frowned. "Do I? You know, all this talk about adjustments, about having to make them when you marry— I can feel myself turning into what you keep insisting that I am. Sort of stately or something. Like I might break. I'm made of meat and bone and muscle, like anybody else. Suppose sometimes I want to whoop or holler? Damnit, I don't want to go through life being too lady-like."

He grinned teasingly. "But you're a lady, aren't you?"

"You honestly don't seem to get what I mean. Look, I can put it another way. Even before your mother flew down last week to drive back with us, something funny was happening to our love-making, my darling. Something I don't think I care for. My God, is it going to degenerate eventually into a formal little ritual run on a time schedule with both of us not daring ever to change the words or the motions, as if it was a—a sacrament or something?"

Her words sounded coarse and made him squirm inwardly. "I was under the impression that everything had been satisfactory," he said stiffly.

"Don't get all hurt, now. In the beginning it was wonderful. And I trusted you and I began to get . . . a lot bolder, if you'll remember."

He remembered and flushed. The crawling, the seeking, and a crazy pleasure that sidestepped across the line into an agony.

"There could have been more and more, my darling. With you I'm a wanton, because I love you, and love can't be pigeonholed into right and wrong. And love can't be fooled, you know. You didn't say anything. But in your body I could feel . . . oh, a sort of withdrawal, and a coolness, and . . . shock, I guess. I wanted us to go on and find a thousand ways to love each other, all of them perfect. But somehow you managed to make me shy again, just when I was getting over being shy, and instead of learning and doing new things, we're getting into a rut, and that isn't what I expected or wanted marriage to be."

"I don't like that kind of talk, Linda."

"Makes you squirm or something, doesn't it? Sex talk in the bright sunlight. Remember those first days in Taxco? You took me in the afternoon. Now the night has become the time for making love. As if it were something shameful to be hidden away in the dark. Don't you like the look of my body by daylight? Are you ashamed of your own? You shouldn't be. One afternoon the sun shone across our bed. Remember?"

He remembered. He remembered his own stallion look and her white knees lifting and the crazy sun madness, and they had laughed.

She moved close to him and touched his wrist. "Darling, it's been worse since your mother came down. All sort of aseptic and nasty."

"I had no idea you felt—"

"Now hush and don't accuse me of anything. I just think, darling, that somewhere inside of you is a little lid that's screwed down tightly on top of some very real honest lusty warmth. For the first days of our honeymoon we managed to loosen that lid a bit and it was very good, for both of us. Then you noticed that too much of you was escaping, so you fastened the lid back down again. And, my darling, I feel left out. I want us to find some way to . . . release you. Sex isn't a nasty word. Neither is breast or buttock or nostril or left wrist. I think somebody gave you the wrong slant when you were a little boy. I certainly don't want to have to learn to think of the

sexual act as a rather quick and unpleasant little wifely
duty to be endured in stoic silence. I want to be a wife,
and a damn good mistress too."

"Please, Linda!"

"Well, I do!"

"And there's such a thing as good taste, you might remember."

"Don't try to feed me that pallid kind of philosophy,
my boy. Just take my word that you're wrong, and that
you can do something about it. I'm nineteen and you're
twenty-two, but this is something you can't patronize me
about, because I think my instincts are right, John Carter
Gerrold."

"Probably all women want the honeymoon to last forever. I hear it's a sign of the immaturity of American
women."

"Nuts! You know what kind of relationship I want
with my man? Read a book by Hemingway. 'To Have and
Have Not.' "

"He writes filth."

"Filth is in the mind of the beholder, darling."

"All his people are Neanderthal."

She looked at him angrily. "You bring up a point. Maybe I have a hunch that if you aren't a whole and uninhib-
ited man in this part of marriage, you might not be much
of a man in anything else. And maybe you'd be better off
trying to do something besides work for your Uncle Dod
for twelve thousand a year when we get back."

"Linda," he said brokenly, "I . . . I hate those things
you're saying, but I can't stand quarreling with you."

She knelt and kissed him quickly, lightly on the lips.
"Poor old Johnny. You just married a wench, that's all. I
look virginal as all hell. That's how come I held my modeling job and how come your family finally relented. But
believe me, honey, I'm going to straighten you out in this
particular department. I want you to promise to try to
help me." She moved a bit closer, thrusting her breast
against his upper arm, turning her body slowly back and
forth, giving him a gamin grin. "You know, it has helped
my shyness a little just to talk it out, Buster."

It made him want her, badly, and at the same time it made him want to move away from the warm insistency of the touch. This was something that she would probably get over, in time. You had a right to be a little crazy on your honeymoon. That didn't mean you had to keep it up forever. He glanced around guiltily to see if anyone were watching them. She sank back to her original position. He wished she would sit up straight. It made her look so damnably hippy to lie like that, even though she was so slim as to look almost fragile. That was another thing that had startled him. He had taken her the first time with almost a fear that he would hurt her, crush her. But her slimness had a muscled vibrancy that had almost shocked him.

She would get over it after a bit and take a proper wifely attitude. If a man had a taste for the more alarming, overpowering indecencies, let him go see some whore. The marriage bed was certainly not an arena for the wanton display of versatility. And experimentation was only necessary to that degree which resulted in the discovery of an effective method.

She seemed to enjoy it too much, and that didn't seem right, somehow.

He wished she would hate it. And then he could feel that almost pleasant guilt afterward, and apologize to her abjectly, and beg her forgiveness for dirtying her.

He glanced down toward their black Buick sedan. "I can't understand why Mother insists on staying in the car. It must be like a furnace."

"She'd rather be in a furnace than take a risk of picking up some Mexican microbe, darling."

"I don't see where you have any right to criticize her, Linda."

"Oh, I know. She's been a swell buddy to you. And she's so terribly conscious of striking exactly the right attitude toward me. John's cute little wife. 'She did some modeling, you know, just as a hobby, for one of the best agencies in New York.' That killed me the first time I heard it. I could lose five pounds during a tough day under those lights, and fall into bed so bushed I couldn't even take time to brush my teeth. The money I made got my brother through his last year of law school. Great hobby."

"I know it does sound a little snobbish, Linda, but you've got to realize that she was raised in the Rochester atmosphere. And she's a very strong and determined woman. It wasn't easy on her when my father left us and ran off with that tramp who worked in his office, either."

She tilted her head and looked at him. "Your father fell prey to the dreadful magic of illicit love?"

"That's right."

"You know, that's a clue I never thought of before. How old were you?"

"I was seven at the time, and I worshiped my father. I don't know what you mean about a clue. It was a terrible shock to me when he went away. I couldn't understand it. I could just get the vague idea that he'd done some nasty thing with a woman, but I didn't know what it was. He wrote pleading letters for years, but Mother refused to divorce him."

"The poor woman."

"Yes, it was hard on her."

"I didn't mean that woman. I mean the one he ran off with."

"If that's your idea of a joke, Linda . . ."

"You better go see how Mother Ann is before I say something I shouldn't."

He walked away from her, holding his back rigid. The stupid ferry seemed to be lodged permanently on the far bank. He looked into the Buick. All the windows were down and the elder Mrs. Gerrold sat in the back seat. She was leaning against the pile of suitcases, sound asleep. Her dress looked damp and her face was shiny with perspiration. Only the crisp gray ringlets of her hair looked undaunted.

John smiled and walked back to his bride. Certainly if Mother had realized how much she would detest Mexico, she would never have flown down to ride back with them.

"She's asleep," he said.

She yawned. "Let's take the blanket and the thermos

and walk down by the river. Maybe we can find a spot
of cooler shade."

She took the thermos and walked ahead of him. The
dress was one he had bought her in Mexico City. It was
a good dress, beautifully fitted across the hips, around
the waist. She walked with the gliding grace of the
trained model, her head high, toeing in slightly, hips
moving tautly compact under the nubby fabric. In childhood imaginings Diana had walked from the garden
pedestal, and had walked exactly that way. They kept
to the high bank and he caught her arm to help her
where it dipped steeply down toward the murky water.

"Want to go wading?" she asked.

"Not in that stuff, certainly. There doesn't seem to be
any place down here. Shall we go back?"

"Let's try along the bank. Come on."

He shrugged and followed her. The sun began to bite
through his thin shirt into his shoulders. Sweat stung the
corners of his eyes.

On and on. "Hey, is this a cross-country hike?"

"Just to there, John. Just to that clump of trees."

"That's another half mile!"

"But it looks so pleasant."

When they got to the trees, he saw that it was pleasant.
These trees were taller, thicker. And the grass was green
under them, not seared and dusty as back by the highway. They sat on the spread blanket and drank spar-
ingly of the water. He looked up across a bend of the
river. The toy ferry twinkled in distant heat. Cars waiting on the far bank sent blue-white dots of chromium
fire across the distance.

"Cooler here, isn't it?" she said.

"Mmmm. Much. You're a bright girl."

She lay back on the blanket and said, "Kith me quick.
I'm thickthteen."

He bent over her and kissed her, lightly. Her arm went
around his neck and pulled his lips back again as he
started to sit up. Her mouth enlarged and was moist.
He liked the light dry kisses. These kisses were the
ones that brought on the need of her, brought on the

spinning craziness. She moaned and thrust against him.

"Now," she said, deep in her throat. "Now, John Carter Gerrold. Here and now, in sunlight again."

"Your dress," he said haltingly. "It will be rumpled. And besides, I didn't . . . I don't have any of . . . "

Her eyes were closed. "That doesn't matter."

"But we were going to wait for a year before we . . ."

Tears squeezed out from under her closed lids. "I thought of that. I have a funny theory. Right now, with what we still have for each other, we can make a baby with eyes that will laugh, a baby to roll brown in the sun, and husky. A year from now, all we can make will be sad-eyed pale little children with . . . with the love left out."

She sat up, frankly crying, hitched the skirt of the dress from under her hips, pulled the dress off over her head, and lay back again, dressed in the blue honeymoon wisps of fragilest nylon and lace.

He took her then, more roughly than ever before, with her responding tautly, with love a pulse like the measured beat of a drum, took her with an almost shocking quickness matched by her own readiness. And while it was happening, while all the world had focused down to the chant of bodies, a kind of singing, he knew that this was right and true and forever, that there was no nastiness, that Diana had been stone, and this was flesh to enclose him tightly.

And they lay side by side, her head tucked against his shoulder.

The uncomfortableness was seeping back, the feeling of having done something animal, reprehensible. The body that had been incredibly lovely only moments before was becoming overpoweringly of the flesh, sticky-soft, enervating.

He said quickly, thickly, "Now is when . . . it happens. I go sour inside. As if it had been wrong. I don't know. Maybe you're right about that lid. Something twisted wrong inside me."

"How much money do we have left?" she asked, surprising him.

"Huh? Oh, maybe four thousand. A little more."

"Darling, Uncle Dod can get along without you for a little time. We'll drive your mother home, and then we're going out to Santa Fe and call on your father and his lady."

He sat up, conscious of nakedness, reaching quickly for his shorts, scissoring his long legs into them. "Mother would *never* permit that."

"Don't you see? This strange sort of reserve of yours comes from what happened. If it had hit you harder, I think you might possibly have turned into a queer, a fairy."

"What a grotesque—"

"Let me finish. The idea was deeply implanted in you that women are something nasty. Loving a woman is faintly unpleasant to you. You love me. So far it has been strong enough, that love, to take good care of us. But unless we go and dig out the causes, we'll never have a good life. Please, John."

"I have nothing to say to him or to that woman. After what they did—"

"Nothing to say to them, but maybe something to learn from them. If their love, legalized or not, has been strong enough to last for fifteen years, I wouldn't be surprised if we found something very special, very refreshing. And I've noticed one thing. You keep saying your father 'ran off' with that woman. According to what I've heard about it, he left with her quite openly after trying for two years to get your mother to agree to a divorce."

"Get your clothes on," he said harshly.

"Cover up the nasty woman. Get her under wraps. I bet you'd put me in a Mother Hubbard if you thought you could get away with it."

"Shut up!"

"You see, the angrier you get, the better my guess seems to be. And here is your ultimatum, John Carter Gerrold! Either we go out there, or I leave you."

"You don't mean that!"

"I mean it with all my heart."

"That's the only thing that would get me out there. The thought of losing you."

"Then humor me."

He forced a smile. "It looks as though I'll have to. Shall we get back?"

"Soon as you zip me up in back, my friend."

He zipped her up, kissed the nape of her neck. They started back toward the distant highway, hand in hand.

THE DARKNESS 31

on. He had the thrill of the soldier of fortune, but too
...it ... he knew ... him to wish to hear any shot

Chapter Three

DEL BENNICKE upended the tepid beer and let it fill
his throat. He lowered the bottle and stared across at
the young girl and boy walking along the high bank,
headed for the river with blanket and thermos bottle.

A nice little bit. He liked the shape and size of her.
A trim little figure and pointy little breasts and a neat
way of walking. The kid with her was a pup. All hands
and feet, gangly with heavy dark-rimmed glasses and a
sort of girlish look around the mouth. Husky enough,
though. Somehow he didn't look as though he'd be able
to take the right kind of care of that little *atsui kenju.*

He scrubbed his lips with the back of a thick brown
hand, tossed the empty bottle into the roadside dust.
Ragged kids scrambled for it, eager for the deposit
money. The victor gave Del Bennicke a white-toothed
grin.

Suddenly, in spite of the heat, Bennicke shivered.
Ye gods, what kind of man could start smacking his
chops over a platinum blonde when all the time he was
carrying around in the back of his mind the picture of
that room in the gook's house in Cuernavaca?

Boy, you really put it in a sling that time. These Latins
can get impetuous, so the man says. He had been in
jams before, plenty of them. But never a daisy like this.
A man in his home town could hardly yak his way out
of this one—and in a foreign county he'd have no chance
at all.

He'd taken the only way out. Left them lying there
and got in the car and headed for the border, the short-
est, fastest way.

Bennicke was a short, compact man with thick shoulders, a wise and worldly tough-nut face, brisk tilted
eyes, and a black brush cut, wiry as horsehair. Wars and
rumors of wars in the earth's far corners had nurtured

him. He had the strut of the soldier of fortune, but too fond a regard for his own skin to wish to hear any shots fired in anger. A brisk line of patter and more brass than a dozen temple gongs had enabled him to worm his way into the homes of the weirder variants of the international set, and be adopted as mascot, drinking partner, or bed companion, depending on the circumstances.

He was a professional guest, and between times he had smuggled gold, worked on oil crews in Venezuela, pimped in Japan. Fists and tongue and knife had got him out of nearly every variety of trouble. He had an ungrammatical flair for languages, came from New Jersey, and thought of all other races as gooks.

And this time trouble had closed in on him, but firmly. Leaving the two bodies behind him, he had boomed up over the mountains through Tres Cumbres and down onto the plain of Mexico City, and the night wind at ten thousand feet had sobered him for the first time in three days. That's where the party had started, in Mexico City. He'd started drinking alone, and by the third drink had picked up an *americano,* a correspondent for one of the news magazines. The *americano* knew of a big party going on among the embassy crowd. They decided to grace the party with their presence. The more tireless members of the party broke off and established a new party in a Chapultepec apartment. One of the drunker citizens was a good bullfighter named Miguel Larra, and he had with him a young item named Amparo, who had just enough *indio* blood in her to make Del Bennicke taper off on the drinking and start a series of oblique maneuvers intended to cut her loose from her bullfighter.

So when the party moved to the bullfighter's Cuernavaca house, Del Bennicke went right along, all of them singing in the big car that swayed and roared across the mountains, with the girl conscious of what Bennicke was up to, and, warm beside him in the car, doing just enough teasing to keep his teeth on edge. It was a big party and it dwindled fast in the big walled house just

north of Cuernavaca as people paired off and/or passed
out. After Larra passed out, Del got to the little girl with
neither more nor less difficulty than he had anticipated,
and found it to be very good indeed, very unusual, and
as torrid as an expert flamenco. And now he knew that
he should have taken off right then and there, hopping
a *turismo* back to the city. But it had been so good he
was thinking in terms of just one more time. "*Solamente
una vez más, por favor.*" But the bullfighter had bounced
back from what should have been a clobbering hangover,
and dragged Del with him down to Lake Tequesquitengo
and initiated him into the art of fishing with goggles and
harpoon gun for large-mouth bass. They picked up half
a dozen bass and drank a large bottle of tequila in
the process and drove back, tight, to Cuernavaca, and
somehow the chance didn't materialize. On the next day,
the rest of the party having faded gently away, the three
of them drove far on dusty roads to look at some bulls
and drink acid pulque, and they got back at dusk, and
Del, bushed and sodden, had hit the sack right way,
only to be awakened perhaps an hour later by the warm
and scented body burrowing against his side like a small
furry animal seeking shelter.

And she had to have a light on, because she was one
of those who has to have a light on, and when she suddenly gasped and stiffened under him, Del turned his
head and saw the bullfighter standing there, face twisted, eyes gone dead, aiming one of the guns they had
used underwater. The short spear with the harpoon on
the end fitted into a slotted tube, and fat rubber bands
slammed it out of the tube. As the rubber bands made
their vicious whacking sound, Del threw himself up and
back, and the thing made a quick gleam in the lamp-
light and chomped into Amparo with a sound that was
both hard and wet. It hit right under her left breast and
she half turned toward the bullfighter. She made the
smallest of gasps and put both hands on the shaft and
pulled at it very delicately, but the barbed head had
turned inside her, precisely as it was designed to do.
She coughed in a most delicate and ladylike way, and

shivered just a bit, and died very quietly, as though to make up by discreetness during her last moments for twenty years of bounding lustiness.

As Del came off the bed, the bullfighter hurled the gun itself and Del eeled away from it and came in fast, thinking only of putting the character out of action long enough to give him time to think. He caught the face with stone fists, and with all the precision he wanted, but with too much panic behind the blows and too much force, and the kiss-off punch lifted the bullfighter's feet from the floor and the first part of him to hit the floor had been the back of his head, and the floor, unhappily had been tile. When Del rolled him over and fingered the back of his head, he felt the sickening looseness. Some piece of the bone must have cut into the brain in a strange way, because during the time of dying the lean bullfighter legs made the same hesitant running motions as a sleeping dog chasing rabbits up the dream hills. The bulls come out of the tunnel into the sun so black that they look like a hole cut from the night. And the running legs could not carry Larra away from the horns of this last bull.

So he had turned out the light and locked the door and later tossed the key into some roadside cactus. It would have been a mistake to take the big car, the one with the horns mounted on front, and the whole car all chrome and a paint the shade of raspberry ice. He had taken the small car and it was British and had no guts under the hood, so it was shifting, shifting, shifting, all the way over the hills and through the night, sober now, and figuring on getting to Matamoros and parking the car in the square and walking across the bridge before the alarm went out and things got warmer than he cared to think about. A jam supreme. Not only kill a bullfighter, which is headline stuff all over Mexico and South America, but chum up with a correspondent, no less, who can fix you precisely in the time and place where it can't be anybody but you. And a servant fingering the brim of the vast hat as he opened the gate to let the little car out, a faint concern in his eyes, wondering if the *americano* was a *ladrón* stealing the *carrito* of the master.

He stood in the sun and smashed his knuckles into his palm and ice water ran out of his armpits and down his ribs. This ferry business made you feel that the hex was really on. By now he should have been across the border. He knew what would happen if he were picked up. Del Bennicke knew the score on Mexican prisons. The American consul would look fixedly in the opposite direction. Tortillas and beans for twenty years. They wouldn't execute him. Slap him in and let him rot. And a funny angle there. The gook prisoners can do handicraft stuff and sell it and get the extra pesos that mean a change in the diet now and again. But American prisoners are forbidden to make any money in a Mexican prison. He knew he'd be one rough citizen to pick up. There was too much of life left. Too many women he hadn't met yet. Too many bottles to uncork. Too many laughs. Too many brawls.

By now the word would be out. He moved into the shade and stood, still sweating. He had to get a good plan and fast. It was going to be dark, at this rate, before his turn came up to cross the river. Darkness might help a little. More freedom of action. The car was dangerous. In darkness, maybe he could switch some plates. Or maybe just take the plates off the Humber and toss them into the brush and abandon it right there. Move down and go across on the ferry as a pedestrian and try to get a ride to Matamoros with some tourists. And, at Matamoros, the hell with the bridge. The big river would be mostly mud bar. Be a wetback.

He had to leave all his stuff in Mexico City. Hadn't dared stop to pick it up out of that crumby room. But the sweaty money belt around his middle was hard-packed with a nice collection of the pictures of Grant. The bearded general added up to six thousand something. Just get across that border and drift west and pick out a good name and slowly get the documentation to back it up, and then stay out of any kind of jam because the prints are on file, have been on file ever since that extortion rap back in '41. This was enough to give a man religion. Maybe it was the end of roaming. Get hold of a gas station or something and pick out some sturdy wench and raise enough kids to look respectable as all hell. Might be a bang in that, having kids. Something new, to do it on purpose.

And he was back in that tiled room again, with those hands pulling so gingerly on the cruel shaft. He knuckled his eyes and held his breath. Maybe they were waiting on the other side of the river. Or maybe the *policía* were screaming up the road from Victoria.

Oh, baby, you're really in the soup this time. Right up to your pointy little ears. Son-of-a-bitch wanted to nail me with that harpoon thing. Should have aimed higher. Hit him too hard. Knuckles still sore. Maybe I ought to move downstream and swim the river and to hell with the car. Wish there was some joker here who looked enough like me. Get him off in the brush and hammer him and lace him up and switch identification.

He sat on his heels in the shade, atop the bank. On the other side he saw a big young girl in a yellow dress. A nice gutty-looking face, and red-bronze hair and a pair of them to make your eyes bulge like a tromped hop frog. He had vaguely noticed her when the blue Cad had joined the interminable line. With a guy old enough to be her daddy. Not married, that pair. Giving each other the stone face, too. He saw her tilt her bottle up, saw her throat work. She lowered the bottle and looked across at him, forty feet away. She set the bottle down, and fluffed at her back hair, and arched her back a little, just enough to push those things out farther than God intended. There wouldn't be any of that in prison. Not a morsel of it. They'd let you dream about it, and that was all. Probably stop that too, if they could figure out how. Sure turned out to be the little dog on the railroad tracks this time.

What the hell cooks with that ferry? He jumped up impatiently and walked down the shoulder of the road, setting his feet down hard.

As he passed a black Buick sedan, he heard a funny

sound. He went on for a few steps and stopped and listened. He heard the sound again. He followed it back to the Buick and looked in. The Buick was the car the platinum piece had come in. He stared at the old dollie in the back seat. Her face was gray and her eyes were open a little and all he could see was whites. Her hands were flexing spasmodically and cords in her throat stood out. The noise he had heard was a startling loud grinding of her teeth. Blood stood bright in the corner of her mouth.

That old doll was really sick. Maybe dying. Bennicke wheeled and trotted through the heat, trotted down to the bank. People looked curiously at a man who would run on such a day. People stood around down by the bank, staring numbly, hopelessly across the river where slow-motion figures swung listless shovels.

Del went over to the two queers who sat in the shade of the MG. One was blond and one was dark, and both of them were pretty. "You boys notice where the girl with the real blonde hair went? Her and her boy friend?"

They stared at him with their shining eyes. The dark one giggled. He said, "They were carrying a blanket and they went thataway, pardner." He pointed downstream.

"Thank you sweetly," Del lisped.

"I suppose you think you're really smart," the blond one in the red silk shirt said.

Bennicke moved down the river bank, keeping to the high ground, looking ahead of him. At last he saw the pair of them coming. He went directly toward them. When he was close enough, he could see that flushed tangled look about the girl, the look of love.

"Say," he said, as they looked at him oddly, "you go with the black Buick with the New York plates, don't you?" The boy nodded. "The old lady in the car is sick or something. Maybe you better hustle and take a look at her."

Without a word the boy brushed by him and began to run, long-legged, fleet.

The girl said, "Thank you very much." She hurried

away after the boy and Del trotted along behind her.
Certainly a cute little figure.

By the time they got to the car a group had gathered.
The boy had the back door open. The woman had
slumped over farther. She was still making that sound.
The boy looked completely helpless, completely stricken.

"Linda, she's . . . she's awful sick. I don't know
what . . ."

Del tilted up his chin and in a brass voice he brayed,
"Is anybody around here a doctor? *Hay un médico aquí?*"
He tried again. The gathered laymen shifted uncom-
fortably, in guilt at not being doctors.

The girl in the yellow dress came down off the bank.
She addressed herself to Del. "No doctor, hey. I don't
know what I can do, but I was in training to be a nurse
before it got too rugged for me."

"Take a look. What do you think?"

The girl had a ripe heavy scent. She pushed by Del
and looked into the car.

"God!" she said softly, reverently. She backed out,
looking pale. "I thought maybe it was heat exhaustion
or something. I don't know what that is. Sort of like a
convulsion or something. Don't think it's a heart attack.
Only thing I can say is to get her out of that oven in
there. If we could fix up a stretcher, like. Then take her
into one of those stores. She better have a doctor quick."

Del turned and found a boy of about thirteen, a boy
whom he had seen in the store where they still had some
beer.

In his ungrammatical rapid Spanish he asked the boy
if there was a doctor in San Fernando. The boy said
there was a very marvelous doctor there who could speak
excellently English.

"Can you swim across the river?"

"It is possible."

Del took out a twenty-peso note, tore it in half, gave the
boy half. "When you bring the doctor back in one of
those small boats on the far shore I will give you this
other piece of the money. If it is very, very rapid, this
thing, I will give you even more."

The boy raced off down the road. The boy with the glasses had come out of his trance of helplessness. He had taken two suit coats out of his luggage and he turned to Del, saying, "If we had some sticks to put through the sleeves . . ."

A nearby Mexican got the idea and raced off toward a truck. He came back with two lengths of heavy bamboo. Del and the boy improvised a stretcher, and it was Del who got into the car, lifted her awkwardly, handed her out toward the boy's arms. She slipped and her dress tore a bit and they got her onto the stretcher, awkwardly. Her white eyes looked up at the blazing sky and her hands still flexed.

Del took one end of the stretcher and the boy took the other. They carried her up to the store. The crowd parted. A counter had been cleared. They hoisted her onto the long counter.

The girl in the yellow dress said, "Maybe some real cold cloths on her head would help. She isn't having those convulsion things, but if we could get a stick or something between her teeth, it might save her tongue a little when the next one comes along."

A short piece of dirty stick was produced. The girl in the yellow dress washed it carefully, and when Del held the woman's jaw open, she got the stick in. The teeth shut hard on the stick, and it gave her a ridiculous look. An aged dog with an arid bone.

The girl called Linda said, "John, darling, he'll be here soon." She went to him, laid her hand on his arm.

Del Bennicke was not a man easily shocked. But what happened then made him feel almost ill. The boy wheeled on the girl and slapped her across the mouth with a full-arm swing, driving her back so that she would have fallen if the end of another counter had not caught her across the small of her back. Her lips were broken and her eyes were wide and dazed.

In shrill hysteria the boy shouted, "You were making me do that while Mamma was here dying! You took me away for that while Mamma was here all alone."

The girl got her balance and pushed herself away

from the counter. She gave him a long look, an oddly sober, unangered look. And then, with her straight back, with her model's walk, she left the store.

The boy called John gradually became aware that everyone was staring at him. There was contempt in all the glances, Del knew. He saw the sick look in the boy's eyes. He put his face in his hands. He turned and moved closer to his mother.

In the silence the teeth began to make a grinding sound against the stick. The boy took her limp hand, held it throughout the convulsive flexings.

"It's going to be O.K., Mamma," he said softly. "It's going to be fine, Mamma."

Del left the store, searched for the tan linen dress and white hair, saw her walking slowly toward the shade. He caught up with her. Her lips had begun to puff. She looked at him with eyes that had gone quite dead.

Del said, "A guy can lose his head when it's his old lady."

"Thanks for the try, my friend."

"Your husband, isn't he?"

"Let's say wasn't he."

"Don't be too rough on the kid. Some guys take a long time to grow up."

"I can't afford to wait for it, Mr. . . ."

"Del Ben . . . son."

"I'm Linda Gerrold. Thanks for taking charge. John was useless."

The girl in the yellow dress joined them. "Hi, folks. I'm Betty Mooney, by the way. I'm trying to remember some of that stuff I tried to learn out of the nursing books. Honey, that jerk certainly teed off on you, but don't let it get you down."

"Miss Mooney, Mrs. Gerrold. And I'm Del Benson. Remember anything out of the books?"

"I got a vague idea of a word. Some kind of hemorrhage in the head."

"Cerebral?" Linda asked.

"Honey, that's exactly it! A stroke, kind of. And if I'm right, there isn't a hell of a lot you can do except

wait and see if she comes out of it. They go into a kind
of coma, and you want to feed glucose and so on, you
can keep them going until they either kick off or wake
up. Lots of times it's better if they kick off when they
have a daisy like that one, because they come out of it
paralyzed. Only I wouldn't tell that kid in there what
I'm telling you. He's nearly lost all his marbles now, it
seems like."

"Thank you very much, Miss Mooney."

"I could be wrong, honey."

Linda sighed. "I better go back and give him a chance
to slap me again. Maybe I can help a little."

She turned back toward the store. Betty watched her
go. "There's quite a gal, Mr. Benson."

"A little beauty, and well set up in the guts department."

"If I'd been tagged like that, that crumby little store
would be upside down by now." She turned and slanted
her eyes at him. They were almost of a height. "Hello,
Benson," she said.

"Hi, Mooney. Where's your fella?"

She gave a suggestion of a sneer. "You mean where's
old sourball? Sitting over there trying to decide whether
to bite himself and die of the infection."

"Those kind go sour when they get enough."

"How about your kind?"

"For my kind there isn't enough."

"We must have gone to different schools together,
Benson."

He gave her a flat-lipped grin, and his mind was
ticking over, very carefully. The old lady's sickness had
opened things up a little. There might be three cars to
play with: the Gerrolds' Buick, the Cad that this Mooney
gal was traveling in, and the Humber he'd taken from
the bullfighter. Maybe a nice judicious trade, just for
the sake of convenience, would let off some of the pressure. And a guy with a girl, even this flooze, would look
better than a guy alone. Maybe it could be worked out
so that he and Betty Mooney would eventually wheel
into Matamoros in the black Buick. If he was any judge,

Betty's friend looked just as anxious to unload her as she was to walk out on him.

"Is that a glint in your eye?"

"I was wondering how a deal like you got tangled up with that Chamber of Commerce type over there."

"It was a mistake, Benson. San Antone was hot and I was bored and I thought well, just once in my life, I might as well kick up my heels."

"Take him good?"

She ran her tongue tip along her lower lip. "I've got about twelve hundred bucks' worth of clothes stashed in that Cad, Benson."

"From me you won't get twelve bucks' worth of clothes."

"We won't call that news, will we? You're too smart to take."

"You got a place in San Antone?"

"Such as it is, and it isn't much."

"Well?"

"Benson, maybe you move a little too fast, huh?"

"Deal it this way. I spring for rent, food, and liquor. Can you cook in your place?"

Her eyes turned wise. "You wouldn't be trying to drop out of sight or anything? I mean if you've got trouble, don't try to hand me any."

"I might have a little, but nothing I can hand you. You'd be clear all the way. This is Mex trouble. Across the line I'm fine. Only I might have to get across the hard way. You know Brownsville?"

"Not too good."

"Two miles north of town on the main drag is a motel called El Rancho Grande. Maybe the old boy could drop you there. I won't have a car."

"Then maybe we walk to San Antone?"

"Maybe we do."

"I've been crazy all my life, so why change now?"

He looked toward the river. Someone was rowing a boat across. Just one person in the boat. Bennicke cursed softly when he made out that it was the boy. He walked down the road with Betty Mooney and got to the bank as the boy pulled the boat up. The boy looked worried.

He said, "Señor, the Dr. Reinares waits for a child to be brought to him. A snake has bitten the child and so he cannot leave. So he suggests that the señora be taken across in this boat and carried to him."

"Does he know it is a rich señora?"

"I spoke of the Buick and of the gems in her rings, señor. He is a man who considers his duty, however."

"What's he saying?" Betty demanded. Del Bennicke told her.

She stared at the filthy boat, at the fish scales, at the floor boards awash. "She can't ride in that, Benson."

Bennicke heard a shout from the far side of the river. The ferry had at last unloaded. A passenger car and a pickup truck crawled up the planks and were blocked on deck. The ferry began to move toward them.

"So maybe we get her into a car and take the head of the line," Bennicke said softly.

Betty looked at the waiting cars. "That," she said, "is going to be a good trick."

Chapter Four

BILL DANTON sat on his heels, sombrero pushed back off his forehead, tiny end of cheap Mexican cigarette pinched carefully between thumb and forefinger. In threadbare khaki work pants and T shirt with a rip in the shoulder, thonged sandals on brown bare feet, he looked no different than the Mexican farm workers he was chatting with. He and his father owned and ran, as partners, a big place near Mante. Cotton and rice. Work on the place had baked him dark. When he stood up, however, there was a rawboned Texan looseness about his big frame that differentiated him from the others.

They sat near the river bank and he had taken a quiet amusement from the *turista* comments on Mexicans in general. He knew that none of them had picked him out as being as much Texan as Mexican. His pickup truck was the second vehicle in line. He had been on his way from Mante to Houston, accompanied by Pepe Hernández, his good friend, to pick up farm-equipment parts from the wholesaler.

When he thought of it at all, which was seldom, Bill Danton sometimes wondered that one person could be, so completely, two people. Dad was responsible for that. Bill's mother had died a year after he was born. At that time Dad had a place in the valley. Mostly citrus, and some land in vegetables. And the house had needed a woman in it, mostly to take care of the little guy. So Dad had hired a slim, timid, wide-eyed Mexican gal named Rosa. Bill guessed that, at that stage, Dad had most of the usual valley prejudice. You used wetback labor when you could get it. It was cheap labor and it made good sense to take them on and hope you could keep them. If you were a "white man" in the valley, it was O.K. to sleep with Mex gals, if your taste ran that way, but you surer than hell didn't marry them.

And so it had taken Dad about two years to get over the loss of his wife, fall in love with Rosa, and marry her. Now Dad could be amused in a quiet way about the way the valley had treated him after that little social error. But he had told Bill in recent years that, at the time, he was pretty bitter about it. And he didn't want any mark left on Bill, or on Rosa's kids. So he had sold out and moved down into Mexico with Bill and the pregnant Rosa. He had bought the spread near Mante, and made application to become an *immigrante*, and after a few years the papers came through, and Dad was a Mexican citizen. It had taken quite a bit of trouble to get Bill established on a *residente* basis, with special permission to work, while still retaining his United States citizenship.

Dad had prospered in Mexico. Rosa gave birth to five children. The big house had always been full of the warmth that comes only from love. Music and much laughter and hard work. Dad had always spoken to Bill in English, and so, when Bill had been sent up to a private school in Houston, and later had gone to Texas A. and M. for the agriculture courses, he had but slight trouble with languages.

And now, at twenty-five, he was perfectly content with his life, perfectly adjusted. His eldest half-sister had recently married and they were building a house on the Danton land. Rosa, at forty-two, was slim as a girl. Dad, burly, white-haired, was head of the local association in Mante, and was looked up to throughout the area.

Bill imagined that one day he would marry. The girl would undoubtedly be Mexican. But he was in no hurry.

Bill had two personalities. As he sat on his heels in the little group, his mobility of face, the quick gestures of his hands were completely Mexican. When he spoke English it was with a lazy slow drawl, with a certain impassivity of face, with slow infrequent gestures of his big hands. He made the switch from one personality to the other without effort, without conscious thought. When he listened to the tourists complain about the reluctant ferry, he was aware that in his American frame

of mind, he would be almost equally irritated. But, as a
Mexican, he knew that since one obviously couldn't carry
the pickup truck across the river on one's back, and since
the men of the ferry were doing as well as they could, it
was wise to relax, to make small jokes. It could take another hour, or another day. *Quién sabe?* The cultivator
and the largest tractor would remain idle for a longer
period. So? When one must wait, it is well to accept the
fact.

Tree shadows were lengthening, and he squinted his
eyes against a swirl of dust picked up by a breeze that
had scudded across the river, ruffling the water.

Pepe came back and squatted beside him. He sighed
elaborately. "One could grow a long beard while waiting."

Bill grinned. "I think Carmelita will still be in Mante
by the time we get back, *amigo*."

"Ai! I concern myself with this delay because I am a
loyal employee, and become accused of the silliness of
love." He changed the subject. "That shouting some
minutes ago was because one tourist lady has been taken
ill, and has been carried into the store."

"Too much sun?"

"Something else, I think. Something bad, with a grinding of the teeth. She is the mother of the young man we
saw, the one with the glasses who walked with the beautiful girl with the light hair. After the mother was carried in, they spoke together and the man with the glasses
struck the girl in front of everyone. It was very ugly and
very curious. I did not understand it. If she is his wife,
he has a privilege to beat her, but it is better done when
alone, I believe. And the boy who swam, he was swimming for a doctor, and came back, you will notice, with
none."

"You are a veritable newspaper, a monster of curiosity.
It does not concern us, Pepe."

"One must move the hours by with more quickness.
And you, I remember, Beel, applied a crude word to the
young lady with pale hair. Thus, I thought you would
wish to know of her problems."

"I merely called her a *pollita*."

"But with a certain licking of the lips, *verdad?*"

The others in the group laughed. Bill stared severely at Pepe. "But it was you, señor, who whistled, *verdad?*"

"Ah, look!" Pepe said. "Approaching is the evil monster of a ferry."

They all watched it, motionless. There was a concerted groan as it nuzzled against the mud when it was still thirty feet from shore. The laborers aboard stared moodily down at the water, then jumped off into mid-thigh water and began rolling it listlessly with their shovels away from the mud.

Bill said, "From now on the progress will be like that of Pepe hurrying to work. One meter each half hour."

He turned his head and saw the thick-shouldered swagger of the hard-faced American with the bristling black hair. The man came down the road with a ripe-looking girl in a yellow dress. He gave the squatting group a casual, insolent glance and walked to the MG, planted his feet, and stared down at the two young men seated in the shadow of the car.

"Boys," he said, "we've got a sick woman up there. You're giving up your place in line so we can get her over to the doctor."

The blond boy looked coldly at the chunky man, turned to his companion, and said, "Troy, dear, are we going to fall for a moldy old gag like that?"

"Come on up and take a look at her, if you think it's a gag, boys."

"It's far too hot to go staggering up that bloody hill."

The girl in the yellow dress stared at them with contempt. She said, "Benson, you aren't going to get anyplace with them. To hell with them. The ferry takes two cars. Let's find out who owns this pickup."

"Betty, let me hammer on these boys a little."

"You get funny with us," Troy hissed, "and you'll get something to remember us by."

Bill, squatting nearby, was lifting a cigarette to his lips. He stopped the gesture as he saw the wink of sun on the knife blade in Troy's hand. Two members of his little group stood up slowly and moved away. They wanted no part of any trouble.

The chunky man made as if to turn away. Then he whirled back and kicked hard. Bill heard the thud of shoe meeting wrist. The knife sailed over the little car and landed on the far side. The two boys scrambled up, chittering and mouthing delicate obscenities. As one of them dived to run around after the knife, the chunky Benson tripped him brutally so that he fell flat and hard in the dust. And Benson went after the blond one, brushing aside the ineffectual hands, hammering with cruelly accurate fists. Bill saw the nose pulped, saw the pink mist of blood spray in the sunlight, saw the boy fall back against the car, sagging.

Bill came up onto his feet, reached Benson in three long strides, deftly caught the arm, twisted it, and brought it up between the man's shoulder blades, holding him helpless.

The man craned his neck to stare back over his shoulder. In crude, rattling, almost verbless Spanish he demanded to know what the hell Bill thought he was doing.

"Giving you a little chance to cool off, man."

"I thought you were spick. Get your goddamn hands off me."

Bill saw that the dark-haired boy called Troy had retrieved the knife. He pushed Benson away from him, releasing him as he did so.

Benson glanced at the knife, glanced at the contorted face of the boy, and backed uneasily away. The boy with the mashed nose was crying.

"You give him a chance," Bill said softly, "he's going to cut you a little." He turned to the boy. "Put the knife away. I'll keep him off you."

Benson cursed him. "You look like a man, at least. What's the matter with beating up a pair like that?"

"They aren't doing you any harm. They're just different from you, man. The lady was right. You could have listened to her. That's my truck. If somebody's pretty sick, we can rig up a place in the bed of the truck and take her across that way."

Bill looked at the girl. She was staring at him in very frank appraisal. There was a measuring boldness in her eyes that made him feel awkward.

"There sure is plenty of you, Texas. Weren't you talking Mex a while back?"

"A buck says he's half spick," Benson said with contempt. "Look at the clothes."

Bill stared mildly at Benson. "One more time you use the word, man, I'm going to pound on you a little."

"Proves I'm right," Benson said with contempt.

Bill addressed himself to the girl. "Miss, is he any kin to the lady that's sick?"

"No, he was just helping out."

"Then you send the woman's kin down here and we'll fix it up about how to get her across. Tell your friend there that we don't need any more big wheeling around here."

Benson and the girl went up the hill. She kept staring back over her shoulder. Bill rejoined the group. Benson's back was rigid with anger as he walked beside the girl. Bill gave the group a complete report on the conversation, with only slight editing. The editing didn't help in Pepe's case.

Pepe said, "Did he use a word of insult, Beel?"

"Yes."

Pepe pursed his lips. "That one is bad. A violent one. A cruel one. It is very clear in his face. You must watch him very carefully. And ah, the little darlings. Look how they share their sorrow."

The one called Troy had brought water, taken a clean cloth from their luggage, and was just finishing tenderly swabbing the face of the one Benson had hit so sharply, the one who still wept, hopelessly.

Their voices came silver-thin through the afternoon air.

"It is broken, isn't it?"

"A beast. That's what he is, a beast. If he's still here, darling, when it gets a bit darker, I shall . . ."

"No, it's done. Don't try to get even, Troy."

"I don't think it's a bad break, Daniel."

"You *know* it's just pulp. Pulp."

"Well, even if it can't be perfectly set, perhaps it will give you an air . . . a jauntiness, perhaps."

"I hate all of them, all of them. And that kind the most, Troy. They have to humiliate us to get even with themselves, you know. It's because they have the same . . . slant on life and won't admit it. So they have to go around being terribly 'he,' strutting and making women. I don't hate him, I guess I'm sorry for him, dear."

"I could just claw out his horrid eyes, really."

"Now you stop fretting. I'm going to be all right. I just feel a little sick from the shock. And *look* at that pretty shirt! You ruined it when you fell."

They lowered their voices a bit and Bill Danton could no longer hear what was said.

"You will take the sick woman across in the truck?" Pepe asked.

"If it will help them."

"The truck can be backed up the hill to the store. Perhaps it will be easier that way."

"Good idea, Pepe. See if you can get some sort of sticks so we can spread that tarp for shade for her."

Pepe stood up. "Here comes the one with glasses, Beel."

The boy was approaching, accompanied by the girl in the yellow dress. Bill stood up and saw her point him out.

The boy stuck his hand out, his air becoming just a bit patronizing as he saw the way Bill Danton was dressed. "Miss Mooney tells me you're willing to help us. My name is John Gerrold."

"Bill Danton's mine. Thought we might rig up something in the bed of the pickup. It's six feet long and she could be stretched out. My friend is going to rig a tarp for shade. Ferry ought to be close enough to shore in another half hour. How is she doing?"

"I . . . I don't know. It's terrible. Miss Mooney has been a lot of help. My . . . my wife is with her now. If only the doctor could have come over here!"

"I'll back the truck up the hill and get her when it's time."

"I had to give the man in the store a hundred pesos

to let her stay in there. He kept saying it was driving all the customers to the other store."

"Don't worry about it. That's more profit than he's made in the last three months."

John Gerrold looked at the dusty truck with evident distaste. He walked over and stared into it. "I'd like to come along, of course, and bring my wife. But that leaves our car over on this side. I . . ."

"You're ahead of me and my friend in line," Betty Mooney said quickly. "Look, I can take that Buick across the river. No trouble at all."

"That's kind of you," John Gerrold said.

"Where will I take it to?"

"They've told me the doctor's office is on the public square, on the left. Apparently he has a sign out. Dr. Reinares. You could leave the car there and bring the keys up to the doctor's office, and then your friend could stop there for you when he gets across. I hope it isn't too much trouble."

"Brother, you're giving me a chance to get off this side of the river. I love you for it."

John Gerrold turned toward Bill. "I'd better get back to her. She's in the first store at the top of the hill. I'll be there with her."

Bill saw the tears gleam behind the lenses of the glasses as the boy turned and looked out across the river. John Gerrold said, "She's always been such a good sport about . . . things like this ferry business. She called them adventures."

"She'll be O.K., Johnny," Betty Mooney said emphatically.

He turned without a word and went striding up the hill, long legs scissoring slowly, head bent.

"Is she pretty bad?" Bill asked the Mooney girl.

"Whatever it is, it sure isn't a common cold. Mamma's boy is giving his wife a hard time. Seems to sort of blame her. And here's a kick, Mr. Danton. That pair are on a honeymoon. With Mamma along. Tie that if you can."

She seemed unwilling to leave. He gave her one of the cheap cigarettes, lit it for her. She took a drag, clutched at her throat, and coughed. "Sabotage!" she said in a husky voice.

"Delicados. You have to get used to them."

She took a second drag, cautiously. "Say, they stand right up and talk back, don't they? You live in Mexico?"

"We've got a farm, my dad and I."

"You make a living off it? I've seen some pretty tired land around here."

"It gets better when you get off the highway. And we're in the flats, so we don't get all the wind and water erosion of the boys who slap those vertical fields against the sides of the mountains."

"Some of those fields that are almost straight up and down look weird."

"Weird, all right," he said quietly. "It takes fifty thousand years for nature to stick a little topsoil on those slopes and nail it down with a decent root system. So some little joker clears it, plants it, wears it out, and it washes away and blows away in three years. Most of the good land in Mexico is washing out to sea. Or blowing up in the air to make pretty sunsets."

"We came through a dilly of a dust storm up in the mountains."

"Treated right, this land will pay off."

"You really knock yourself out when you think about it, eh?"

He gave her a slow grin. "Take it a little serious, I guess."

"What do you think of that Benson?"

"Friend of yours, isn't he?"

"No. I just met him when the old lady got sick."

"Why do you want to know what I think of him?"

"Well, you pushed him around a little."

"I guess I just don't like that kind of guy very much. Those boys weren't hurting him any. He just likes to beat on people."

Pepe came over and said, "Observe the tarp, Beel."

"That's good. Let's back it up the hill. Wait, I'll back it up. You stay here and make certain no one tries to steal our place. Want to ride up, Miss Mooney?"

"I'll walk, thanks."

Bill swung the truck out of line, put it in reverse, leaned out the door, and backed it up the hill. There was more blue in the tree shadows, and some of the brassy look had faded out of the sky.

Chapter Five

As THEY had made the turn off the Pan-American Highway at Victoria, to head toward Matamoros, the police sedan had halted them.

The twins, Riki and Niki, in the back seat of the big gun-metal Packard convertible, had been amusing themselves with a bottle of golden tequila, and had been passing it up to Phil Decker just often enough so that he made a serious attempt not to breathe into the face of the mustachioed cop.

Phil's kitchen Spanish turned out to be pretty inadequate and the cop had no English, and so the cop had taken them across to a restaurant where there was a man with respectable English.

When he got the word, Phil held a conference with the twins. They were identical twins, a pair of sleek show-girl blondes wearing identical blue denim play suits. Tequila had made the four blue eyes a bit glassy.

"Like this," Phil said. "There's some kind of delay at the ferry about a hundred miles down the road there, and the cars are getting across too slow. If we stay at the hotel here, we can probably get across in the morning with no trouble. Or we can go to Laredo to cross, which is no dice on account of the one-week stand near Harlingen. We stay overnight, we got to fly like big birds to get settled in and straightened away from Harlingen tomorrow night."

"Woops, we're marooned," said Riki.

"We can take a chance on the ferry, but when these kids say something is bad, it's usually worse."

Niki turned owlish. "Think of our public, Phil. Leave us lay in supplies, advance on the ferry, and picnic as we wait. A hundred miles from now some of the sting ought to be out of this sun."

The suggestion was carried by a vote of two against one, the twins against Phil, and with resignation he pro-

53

cured a picnic of sorts from the hotel. When he got back to the car he found that Riki and Niki had done a bit of foraging, and the bottle supply was once again up to par.

As they had started down the highway, the twins had started to sing again. There were not enough of them, nor was there enough quality, to make it come out Andrews or Fontaine, but it came out lusty, with a nice drive to it.

Phil Decker drove doggedly. The long run at the Club de Medianoche had filled up the kitty, and Sol had lined up enough stands between the border and New York so that they ought to be able to arrive with the kitty maybe a bit bent but not busted.

And this time, he told himself grimly, they were going to make the TV idea work. Sell it to somebody. The kids were young and had talent. And he wasn't getting any younger. The routines would have to be cleaned up, but that wasn't hard. Wangle a few guest spots, and pray. This time the Triple Deckers ought to come through.

He had no illusions about himself. He knew he was a baggy-pants comic with an ugly face, a heavy left hand on the piano, and a sense of timing and pace learned the hard way, learned in crumby clubs from border to border. It was the kids who were going to clinch it for him. A piece of luck finding the kids right when Manny got so sick and had to quit. A pair of Cleveland gals who'd won an amateur contest and had been booked around with a poor act of their own devising. He'd watched them, made the offer, sewn them up, gone to work on them. Now they had a bag of tricks. The gutty singing, and the duet strip. It had been tough talking them into the strip, but after they'd gone through the paces that first night in New Orleans, awkward and damn near blushing all over, the gals had been convinced that he was right. And they had the milkman skit, and the sorority-house skit, and that blackout business with the violin. A fast, rough show, with plenty of long slim legs, and plenty of double-talk that wasn't too coarse.

Well, this was going to be the gamble. The big time, or crawl away on your belly, Phil boy. And the nagging fear came back that maybe the gals had too much class. Somebody would step in and take over and cut him out. Well, the contract was as tight as he could make it, and they'd have to do a lot of scrambling around, but if they wanted to get out of it, they could probably fix it up somehow. He had learned about contracts the hard way, too.

There was one way you could tell real class when you ran into it. Riki and Niki were not going to let anybody's bed get in the way of ambition. They never let themselves get separated, and the two of them could certainly handle any pair of eager guys.

He realized he had made a fool of himself in New Orleans, but it had worked out all right. He certainly hadn't wanted to mess with either or both of them, because he knew that could foul up an act quicker than anything. And he knew that neither of them had intended to tease him along, but living like that, having to go into their room, having them get so casual with him that it was as if they thought he was one of those boys they fix up so they won't make trouble around a harem—it had got a little too much to take. And so he'd made that fast pass at Niki and she'd blown up in his face and there had been a lot of yammering and then the big conference, at which he apologized very abjectly and they promised to comport themselves in such a way that he wouldn't be so likely to lose control in the future.

They had been good for quite a while, but lately they'd been getting careless again. Now it didn't seem to bother him so much though. He guessed he was worrying too much about how they'd do in New York. Or maybe just getting too damn old. In the Mexico City hotel he'd been talking to Niki one afternoon and Riki had come out of the bathroom wearing a big yellow towel knotted around her waist. Riki hadn't seemed to be aware of herself, and you couldn't blame the kid, because there is certainly nothing like a strip routine done for better than a year to make a shambles out of the modesty department. But Niki had remembered and told Riki to go put something on, and Phil had heard himself saying that it didn't make any difference. But she went and put a robe on anyway.

Good kids, and once they'd had a chance, they began

to show a natural instinct for timing. Hell of a job at first, because they kept throwing away the best lines, and chopping laughs right down the middle. Had to start right from the beginning. Teach them how to walk as if they were coming down the ramp at the Diamond Horseshoe. Teach them how to push the voice out from the diaphragm, push it out round and heavy enough to bounce off the far corners of the noisiest joint. Riki had a nice talent for the dumb-blonde routine, wide-eyed, mouth a button of shock and surprise. Niki could do the best with a suggestive leer. The Mexican customers as well as the tourists had eaten it up.

The routines would have to be cleaned up a bit. That wouldn't be hard. He hoped they would photograph right for the TV cameras.

Might be able to do something with that knack of Niki's to imitate people. They were singing again. One of them, he didn't know which one, leaned forward from the back seat and handed the bottle to him.

Funny how they both started tapping the bottle at the same time. No harm yet. Always sober at showtime. Made you worry a little bit, though. Maybe something was nibbling on them. Something they hadn't mentioned.

They seemed happy enough. Maybe a little wackier than usual, if anything. The drinking had started about the time that big bruiser had taken a shine to Riki. What was his name? Roberts. Robertson. Something like that. Skipped from Boston to play in the Mex league. A pitcher.

Hell of a thing if one of the twins should fall in love right now. Ruin everything. That night, a week ago, when he went by the room. It could have been one of them crying.

He took a second little knock at the bottle and handed it back. "Take it easier on the singing," he said gruffly. "Don't want you hoarse in Harlingen."

"Are you a little hoarse in Harlingen?" Riki asked.

"Me, I'm a big sheep dog in Denver," Niki replied.

"Yuk, yuk, yuk," Phil said sourly.

"That's his trouble. No sense of humor. Old Mother Decker."

"Old Mother Phil. How about this? Old Mother Phil went up the hill, to get his poor girls a laugh. And when he got there . . . hmmm . . ."

"The hilltop was bare."

"And so were the girls."

"Hey, it's got to rhyme, you," Riki complained.

"So what rhymes with laugh?" Phil asked.

"Would giggle be better?" Niki asked.

"Try grin. Then you can use gin. Speaking of gin, Mother Decker, how about another kick?"

"Another knock and we all ride in the back seat. Want me to roll this wagon in this countryside?"

Niki stared out the window. She said in an awed tone, "The land that Charles Addams forgot."

"Hey, write that down," Phil said. "Put it in the ad-lib book. We'll use it for snow blindness. You know. Empty joint. Cold crowd. 'Is that a vulture sitting up there?' Niki says, looking up, kinda, shading her eyes. We won't use Addams. Maybe Boris Karloff. Something about him forgetting it or something."

"Or a crack about the food in whatever joint it is. Too rough?" Riki asked.

"Too rough. Let's work it around somehow. There's a gag there someplace."

The top of the car was up, as protection against the blistering sun. The back window was unzipped. A pair of red sandals followed by long lithe legs came sliding over into the front seat.

"Getting dull back there," Niki said. "Girl back there thinks she looks like me." She braced the red sandals against the glove-compartment door.

"Everything O.K. with you two?" Phil asked.

"We don't make much money, but we have a lot of fun."

Phil looked in the mirror. Riki had spread herself out on the back seat to take a nap. Niki, beside him, squinted straight ahead at the highway, no expression on her face. Both girls' hair was tied back with red ribbon that matched the sandals.

"We're going to kill them in New York."

"Sure, Phil."

"You got nerves about it?"

"Not a nerve in my head, lambie. Supremely confident, that's me."

He had to be satisfied with that. But he still didn't feel quite right about the pair of them. Somewhere in the immediate past he had lost control somehow. There was something on their minds, something they hadn't told him yet. He crossed mental fingers. Here he was with roughly two hundred and forty pounds of female talent, bursting with health and bounce. Enough to make a man suspicious. How lucky could you get? Too lucky, maybe. Hell, one little phone call to Sol and he could put the Triple Deckers into a Bourbon Street joint from now until Dewey turned Democrat. Maybe that would be the thing. Stick to small time. Forget how the pair would look on a Life cover.

The miles swept at them and were snatched under the droning tires. They topped a small rise. Phil pumped the brake and they eased to a stop behind a blue Cad. A long line of cars and trucks stretched down the hill to the river bank.

"This is the picnic grounds, ladies," Phil said. "Here in this natural retreat, surrounded by the beauties of nature . . ."

"And house flies."

". . . you will drink in the mysteries of . . ."

"Who said drink?"

Niki and Riki piled out, stretching long cramped legs. They attracted, as usual, open-mouthed attention. When Phil had first taken them in tow, they hadn't known how to handle themselves while being stared at. They had just been a pair of corn-fed beauties who happened to be twins. Now no one could doubt for a minute that they were in show business. They had the air and the walk, and as far as the stares were concerned, they might just as well have been absolutely alone. They'd never given up their cute trick of walking hand in hand, and Phil hadn't made them stop it. They told him they were going exploring. He got out of the car and watched them going down the dusty road, hand in hand, heads shining in the slant of the late-afternoon sun. He decided he was very proud of them.

He saw them move to one side to get out of the way of a pickup truck that was backing up the hill. The truck backed all the way to the end of the line, then swung down through a shallow ditch and up to the front of a tired-looking little store.

A tall young guy in glasses came trotting out, glanced at the truck, and trotted over to Phil. "Are you a doctor?" he demanded.

"No, son. Sorry."

The boy turned on his heel and ran back to the store. There was quite a crowd around, staring in the door. Phil walked over to see what was going on. The big fellow who had driven the truck had gone into the store. As Phil got closer he heard some crisp Spanish and the crowd got out of the way a bit. The big guy and the young fellow came out carrying a stretcher made of a couple of coats buttoned around bamboo poles. There was a gray-haired lady on the stretcher. Phil guessed that if she were awake and on her feet, she'd look like quality.

She certainly looked sick. Face like a washrag. Phil swallowed hard. That was the way Manny had looked when the ambulance came after him. And it made him remember that he was exactly Manny's age. Forty-nine. The gals thought he was forty-two. Stop using the little brush and the bottle, and his hair would probably be the same color as the lady on the stretcher's. Damn hard to be a comic, to think of the punch lines, to dress up the routines, when way down in your mind you kept thinking of death. The years go by so damn fast.

The crowd was very still. Kids watched, wide-eyed. A Mexican slowly took off his big straw hat and then made the sign of the cross. The two men eased the stretcher onto the truck. The boy scrambled in with blankets, awkwardly wedged them under her.

The big Mexican fellow looked around. He turned to Phil and the Texas drawl startled Phil considerably as he said, "If you could back that car of yours up, friend, I could drive out to where the ditch isn't quite so steep."

"Sure," Phil said. "Sure thing."

He went to the car and backed up, giving the truck plenty of room. There was a little girl in the truck now, too. A pretty little bit. Silver-colored hair and a trim little figure. Looked like somebody had given her a bust in the mouth not too long ago. But he couldn't imagine anybody doing that. Probably she fell.

The big fellow tooled the truck through the ditch, creeping it along. When it turned down toward the ferry, Phil moved the Packard up to the back bumper of the Cad and turned it off. He pocketed the key as he got out. He stood, blinking in the sunlight, a small worried-looking man with clown lines around his big mouth, with simian forehead, wearing an absurdly unsuitable pair of maroon shorts with wide white bands down the side seams. His two girls were two dots of pale blue beyond the dust. Phil hiked up his maroon shorts and set off down the road. He had learned, early in life, how to case a house. This one was a crazy mixture. He hoped he'd never have to play to a house like this one. Some round, glint-eyed little Mexican businessmen. A mess of *paisanos*. A chunky American who looked like a pro athlete of some sort. Another American looking like a banker, sort of a sad-eyed guy. A big redhead with a yellow dress about to bust in front. Some farmery-looking guys. A big tourist family with a swarm of bratty kids. All of them piled up here, just as they'd come along the highway. Down at the head of the line he found a couple of sour-looking flits, one of them with a flattened nose. Recently done. He wondered why people had been getting pounded around here.

The ferry seemed to be stuck so that it couldn't get close enough to shore. They were propping long heavy planks from the end of the ferry to the shore, blocking them up.

He stood in the road and stared at the ferry. Suddenly he heard a loud frightening roar behind him. He looked quickly back over his shoulder, and then made a wild sprawling leap for the side of the road. The front left fender of the big black sedan didn't miss him by more than six inches as the horn blared insolently.

Phil sprawled in the dust. A sharp rock cut his scrawny bare knee. He got up, grunting with anger. He inspected the knee, and then marched down to where the black sedan had stopped. There were two identical sedans.

Phil marched to the driver of the first one. He didn't stop to notice that the man was Mexican or that he was in uniform. Phil planted his feet and yelled, "You tryn a kill me, hah? You nuts or something?"

The driver didn't even turn his head to look at Phil. Two men got out of the other side of the car and came around to him. Phil turned on them and said, "Tell your pointy-headed driver that I got a notion to . . ." His voice dwindled off as he noticed that both these men were Mexican, that they both had broad faces, broad shoulders, annoyed expressions, and guns on their hips.

"All I'm trying to say," Phil said more gently, "is that it looked to me as though that jerk behind the wheel was . . ."

A big hand was placed flat against Phil's chest. He went sharply backward and sat on the seat of his pants some six feet away. It was not only an indignity. It hurt like hell. He felt as though he had hit hard enough to fracture something. The hefty men turned their backs on him. Others got out—of the same type. He was ignored. They chatted. In the back seat of the lead sedan sat a massive man, white hat brim exactly level above sleepy eyes, ponderous belly resting on his thighs.

Riki and Niki helped him up, one on each side.

"Darling, he hurt you!"

"I don't exactly feel kissed. What the hell's going on?"

He saw some of them turn and stare at him, supported on either side by a tall blonde. They looked amused. His restless mind started to twist the situation into a possible visual gag. If anything could amuse those gorillas, it must have a slant.

He felt tenderly of his poorly padded posterior and arched his back. "Unhand me, gals. Those kids don't play, do they? Hey, look at all those Mexicans coming around to goop at the big boy in the back seat. Who is he, anyhow? The Mexican Gary Cooper?"

The boards had been blocked and the first car of the two aboard the ferry began to inch its way gingerly down.

Phil noticed that all of the men seemed to be armed. He noticed the low numbers of the licenses on the black sedans. Light dawned.

"Gals," he said firmly, "that guy is a politician. Remember the one who came into the club? Yessir. A local Mr. Big."

Chapter Six

WHEN Bill Danton, the lanky Texan, saw the two black sedans come roaring down the road, saw the horn blast the sparrowy little man in the red pants into the ditch, he had a sinking feeling that seemed to be centered around his heart.

He saw the little man object, saw him knocked down, saw the flamboyant twins pick him up. Then Bill moved to where he could look into the lead car, see the face of the man on the back seat. And he knew that there had been nothing wrong with his hunch. The fat sleepy man would no more wait a turn in line than he would try to fly like a *zopilote*, one of the big circling buzzards.

Bill drew back into the natural manner of any Mexican when confronted with a powerful and unscrupulous fellow citizen. He gave all of his attention to the cigarette he was smoking.

John Gerrold jumped down and came around to the front of the truck. His eyes looked a little wild. "What's all this about? Why didn't they stop at the end of the line? What are they doing down here?" His pale-haired wife appeared beside him. She too was looking anxiously at Bill.

"I think they get the next ride across, Gerrold. I don't think there's anything anybody can do about it."

"What gives him the right? Who does he think he is?"

"He's the head of a new political party in the northern provinces. His name is Atahualpa. That's not his real name, of course. It's the name of the last Inca king. He claims to have some Inca blood, though I never heard of any Incas in Mexico before. His party is based on some pretty rugged racial ideas. He's nearly pure *Indio*, and ruthless as they come."

"Are you trying to say we won't get my mother across to the doctor on this trip?"

"I've been watching the river. It isn't dropping so fast now. Maybe this round trip will only take fifteen minutes."

John Gerrold turned on his heel and walked toward the group of men. Bill called to him sharply.

John Gerrold had to stop so that the first car that had come off the ferry could pass. The people in the car grinned and waved and shouted as it sped up the hill.

John Gerrold tried to edge by the circle of men, tried to get close to the lead sedan. He was grabbed and spun back. He poised and leaped at them, swinging his fists blindly.

Bill saw it happening, and he was powerless to stop it. He saw the short vicious chop of the barrel of a revolver. He heard the crisp sound as it met bone. John Gerrold stood quite still for a moment, turned half away, and went down onto his face. The bent glasses skittered a few feet in the dust. One lens was shattered.

His young wife ran to him, knelt beside him. The men moved away as though a bit embarrassed. She gently rolled John Gerrold over onto his back. Bill saw that Atahualpa had not even turned his head.

The girl looked toward Bill and cried out, "Can't you do something?"

Bill was conscious that all the spectators had moved back. He felt that he was very much alone. There was the very real chance that Atahualpa would continue to gain power in the government, and he would make a very bad enemy of the Danton family. Obscure rules could be applied. It was even possible that, should Atahualpa achieve real power, the citizenship of Bill's father could be canceled on some technicality, that the wide rich lands of the Rancho Danton could be handed over, almost for nothing, to Atahualpa.

Logic said to lay low, make but the smallest of sounds. Bill was not the least naïve about Mexican politics. Both he and his father were conscious, always, of the threat hanging over them—threat of a change of regime, a change of viewpoint toward *norteamericanos* that would make their life impossible.

But the girl's fine eyes were on his, in helplessness and in appeal. And his father had said, many times, "When you have to do something right, boy, don't stop to count how much money you got in your pants."

Bill walked forward, conscious of Pepe, behind him, saying softly, "No, *hombre!* No."

Atahualpa's guard watched Bill's approach with that mild curiosity of a pack of village dogs seeing a strange car coming down the village street. They shifted a little.

Bill stopped, raised his voice, and said, "Was Atahualpa responsible for that stupidity?"

Three of the guards moved lightly toward him, converging. Bill stood tense. When, from the corner of his eye, he caught the flick of the descending blow, he snapped his head away, felt the stir of the heated air against his cheek. The force of the blow spun the man off balance, and as he took a lurching awkward step, Bill struck down at him with a sweeping backhand blow of a big right fist. It hit the guard behind the ear, driving him down into the dust.

The nearest man gave a grunt of anger and the sun gleamed blue on barrel steel. To Bill all movement became stickily slow, as though the low sun and the blue shadows formed some underwater scene. It was incredible that these guards should have such colossal indifference to the law that they would shoot him, kill him here in the dusty sunlight. And he knew at once that it would be written off as a fanatic's attempt against the life and person of Atahualpa, prevented by his brave guards.

He moved in, ducking low, striking upward at the gun arm, feeling that the portion of a second was stretched out like rotten rubber, would break with the impact of the slug against his face. And the gun hammered the air beside his face, blasting his eardrum, leaving a ringing, frozen silence.

He stood on his ties, feeling the aim of another gun close to the small of his back, wanting to cry out that had he known how bold the guards of Atahualpa had become, he would never have bothered them, never.

And a deep voice with a bullfrog thrum in it commanded the guards. They grasped Bill's arms and ran him up to the car, ran him there with such energy that he craned his head back as his chest struck the top of the door frame. They pulled him back a bit, so that he could see into the car. Atahualpa sat in the precise middle of the back seat. His belly bulged against the white cotton outfit, the pajama suit worn by workers in the fields. Underneath the level brim of the spotless white sombrero, the eyes, imbedded in dark pockets of flesh, showed nothing, neither anger nor curiosity nor amusement. They were merely eyes. Organs for sight. As the eyes of any creature in the brush. Hands and wrists, heavily haired, rested on the blocky knees, made childish by the weight of the belly, carried like a sack against the thighs. A bright serape, neatly folded, lay on the seat beside him.

"You know Atahualpa and yet you dared speak in that fashion," the voice rumbled.

Bill began to understand how this illiterate *indio* had achieved so much power so quickly. There was a brutal, elemental thrust to his personality.

"Because I thought Atahualpa was not a fool, I spoke in that fashion." Bill did not use the slurring idioms of the fields, but the crisp precise Spanish of the cities.

The guard on his left twisted his wrist cruelly, bending it back. Bill felt the gasp build up in this throat, but shut his teeth hard against any such fatal show of weakness.

"Perhaps it can be explained why it is foolish to fend off the attack of a stupid young *turista*."

"It was not an attack. The mother of the foolish young man is unconscious in the back of that truck. He is desperate to take her across to the doctor in San Fernando. He saw you usurping his rightful turn to cross the river. The ill woman and her son are rich important citizens of the Estados Unidos."

"I do not wish the good wishes of that imperialist nation, or of the *turistas*. The *turistas* have made our money cheap. My people suffer."

"This is not a talk of politics, Atahualpa. This is a talk of mercy. But as you wish to speak of politics, I must ask if Atahualpa wishes to be known as the man who let an elderly señora die because he pushed ahead of her in line? Or as the man who caused an official protest to be made to the *presidente?* I had thought you were not yet strong enough to attract so much attention, señor."

Atahualpa looked at him steadily for long seconds. He gave an order to one of the guards. The man trotted over, stared into the back of the truck, trotted back, and said, "It is the truth."

"Who are you?" Atahualpa asked gently. It was the question Bill had dreaded.

"The younger Señor Danton of Mante."

For the first time there was a flicker of expression in the man's eyes. "Indeed? The Rancho Danton is a rich place. You dress poorly. But I see you have a gringo arrogance."

"Matched by the arrogance of your guards, who would kill without question."

There was another quick order. The men released Bill's arms. He carefully tested his left wrist. It was painful, but apparently not sprained.

Atahualpa leaned over, grunting, and fumbled with something at his feet. He came up with a cheap plastic mechanical pencil. It was the sort given away by the tens of thousands by United States firms. In an imperious manner he handed it through the window. Bill took it, curiously. He looked at it. On the pencil was printed, "A Friend of Atahualpa." He wanted to laugh. He wanted to laugh so hard that he would drop in the dust, hugging his sides and gasping. He knew his face was reddening.

"Do not say that Atahualpa cannot recognize a service, Señor Danton. You will keep the pencil in a safe place. Atahualpa never forgets a service."

Bill managed to bow and say grave words of thanks and appreciation.

Atahualpa gave a quick order. The man who had fired the shot turned and tried to run. The others caught him. It was very quick, merciless, brutal. Bill turned his eyes from it and saw the young Mrs. Gerrold do the same. Pepe watched with a look of horrified fascination. When the thick wet sounds of blows had ceased, the gun and gun belt were placed in the second car. The unconscious guard's pockets were slashed and his few pesos removed. He was dragged diagonally across the road, across the gray mud, and pulled out of sight behind the brush.

"There are many others who are eager to serve," Atahualpa murmured to Bill. "Who will accompany the sick señora?"

"Her son, of course, and the wife of the son, the girl with the *pelo blanco.*"

John Gerrold had regained his senses. He got weakly to his feet, wiping at the thin line of blood that ran down behind his ear into his shirt collar. He leaned quite heavily against his wife, and his eyes were dazed.

When the guards took the stretcher from the truck, John Gerrold made a hoarse protest. Bill grabbed his arm and said in a low tone, "Look, this is O.K. You and your wife are going along. He'll see that you get to the doctor. Just keep your mouth shut."

The unconscious woman was placed, with great tenderness and many sounds of sympathy, in the back of the second car. The displaced guards got into the lead car. The young couple was ushered politely into the second car.

Atahualpa leaned toward the window. "Señor Danton, the doctor will be advised that it will be unlucky for him if he is not able to make the señora well."

"I am deeply grateful."

"I am grateful to you, señor."

The big cars crawled up the blocked planks onto the ferry. The crew removed the planks with astounding dispatch. Crossing the narrow river, the men pulled so energetically on the tow cable that the heavy craft made a perceptible bow wave.

Bill watched closely as it reached the far shore. This time when it stopped, it seemed closer than on the last trip. Shovels flashed in the sun. Men worked like maniacs. The black sedans were like beetles that glittered.

"Boy, you got more guts than sense," a voice said.

Bill turned and looked down into the tough face of the man called Benson. Benson seemed genuinely awed. Bill said, "I had a little luck, too. I didn't know I'd get shot at.

I thought the worst I could get would be a good beating."

"What the hell did he give you?"

Bill showed him the pencil. "This."

"I'll be plain damned! A two-bit pencil. Friend of Atahualpa, eh? Just like a big greaser. Brother, you seem to know this country pretty well. I'd think you'd know that these gooks would just as soon kill you as look at you once they get big enough to wear guns."

Bill looked at the man and looked away. He knew the hopelessness of ever trying to reach the closed mind, of ever trying to explain that there are no people in the world more innately decent and courteous than the Mexicans. True, it was a country of poverty, of great hardship. But out of that poverty were coming men who were truly great, as well as social cancers like the *indio* calling himself Atahualpa, teaching his policy of hate, of blind racial nationalism.

You could almost see the roots of men like Atahualpa being nurtured in the Mexican ghettos of the towns of the Río Grande Valley. Men like Atahualpa would gain their strength in the northern provinces, where the border tension was a thing that could be felt as easily as the hot weight of the sun.

No, you couldn't take a man like Benson down the main street of the village near Mante, just when the dusk was royal blue, and have him see anything but filth. The huts were small, with packed-dirt floors. Women's hands slapped in endless rhythm at the tortillas, and in the dusk there was love and contentment, a quiet peace of the soul.

Men like Benson would think Mexico was ageless, static, sitting forever wrapped in dreams of *mañana*. But Bill knew well the truly enormous strides that had been made in the last decade. Education, reclamation, industrialization. Truly, it was a race against time. The *comunistas* bred in discontent, like flies in offal. *Turista* arrogance created no love for the powerful neighbor to the north. But if the great men of the nation could move fast enough, could do enough good in the limited time left, then Mexico, a giant awakening, could take a true and strong place in the ranks of the democracies.

Bill shivered with reaction. There was still a shrill whining whistle in the ear that had been too close to the muzzle blast. He could take no pride in having done what was, basically, a foolish thing. It could have destroyed in a few minutes what Dad had taken twenty years to build. And yet, with an incredible luck, he had come out of it labeled Friend of Atahualpa. Something in a girl's grave eyes . . .

He felt as though this incident had caused an odd awakening. Something in his brain had shifted a bit, formed a new pattern. He wondered if he would continue to be as content as he had been before, content with the work and the planning at the *rancho*.

Benson had wandered away. Pepe moved close to Bill. "I shall now die before my time, *amigo*. There is a damage to the heart."

"To add to the damage already caused by a lady."

"I do not believe it wise to tell your father, Beel."

"I will tell him. It is a thing he should know."

"Ai! A nice little trip for parts for the machines. I am quieting my nerves by observing the tall twins with the blonde hair. Such statues. Such splendor! How is it possible that they should belong to the little man with the crooked face?"

"Perhaps he has great wealth. Or it was not permitted to break up a set."

"When the trouble came, the twin girls looked on with excitement, and yet a certain calmness. The little man with the crooked face disappeared behind a tree, very wisely, I thought."

"And you?"

"There happened to be a wrench on the floor boards of the truck. It jumped into my hand. Believe me, I did not pick it up. I do not know why I held it. Had they killed you, it would have impeded the speed of my running. The two little darlings of the small automobile left quickly and have not returned. She of the yellow dress dodged between the cars. The hard little man with the wicked face dropped flat in the ditch at the sound of the shot. Everyone was wise except you, Beel."

"And now I am a Friend of Atahualpa. Let us see if we can help the guard who was beaten."

They went to him. Some children stood at a respectful distance, gravely watching the unconscious man. His face was a bloody ruin. They took his arms and dragged him well into the shade. He groaned and put his arms across his eyes.

"How do you feel?" Pepe asked.

The injured man uttered an obscenity.

"Obviously," said Pepe, "his mind is undamaged. The pattern of his thoughts is unchanged."

The man suggested in a ragged voice that both Pepe and Bill depart for the purpose of committing impossible acts on themselves. Pepe shrugged. They left him there, in the shade, the children still staring at him.

The two boys had come back to their MG. They looked cool, haughty, as though they had arrived at some new mental attitude that enabled them to feel completely indifferent to their surroundings. The face of the injured one had become swollen and dark in the area of the broken nose. It was evident that he would have, quite shortly, two stupendous black eyes.

Bill looked across the river. The planks had been set in place and he saw the second car dip cautiously down, gain the foot of the opposite road, and follow the other one up into San Fernando, in a swirl of dust.

"At last," said Pepe, "it appears that we may one day cross this mightiest of raging torrents. And when we are old men, we shall reach Houston. And by the time I return, I will find that my beloved has married a rival and borne seven children."

The two blondes in their denim play suits and red shoes approached Bill and Pepe.

"Do you speak enough English to tell us what was going on?" one asked.

"Just a little political discussion," Bill said.

"Is anybody going to do anything for that man behind the bushes, or do they just let him lie there and bleed?" the other one asked indignantly.

"Let him bleed," said the little man with the crooked

face. "Friend, that sounded like Texas talk. Let me introduce myself. Phil Decker. These are my partners, Riki and Niki. We're the Triple Deckers. Been playing the Club de Medianoche. Bet you've heard of us. Got a good play in the Mexico City papers."

"We live out in the sticks," Bill said apologetically.

"What was all the shooting about? Shooting makes me nervous."

"Just a little mistake, Mr. Decker. My name's Danton. Bill Danton." He turned to introduce Pepe, but Pepe had wandered discreetly away. He stood by the truck looking fondly at the two sets of long slim legs under the blue play suits.

"We're number twenty-three or so in line, Bill," Decker said. "How long do you think we'll be stuck here?"

"Looks to me like the river has stopped dropping. If the current doesn't fill up those holes they've dug, they ought to get back on a regular schedule. Say, offhand, ten minutes for each trip."

"Four hours, maybe? Say now, that's all right. Listen, gals. It's a little after four now. We'll be across around eight, be in Harlingen by midnight, anyway."

One of the blondes was staring across the river. Shouts came thinly through the air. Shouts of warning.

"What goes on over there?" the girl asked.

They all stared over. A gray truck was lumbering up the planks. The motor was racing, but it didn't seem to be making any progress. Then, looking like a child's toy in the distance, it swiveled a bit to one side. The back end dropped abruptly. They heard wood ripping and splintering. The front end of the truck lifted a bit, wheels turning slowly, and then the whole thing dropped over onto its side. Muddy water shot out in a high hard spray. There was silence and then more shouting.

"That really does it," Bill said softly. "That does it good. Damn fool raced his motor and spun his wheels on the planks and she went off. Couple of tons of truck plunk on its side right in the way. Mr. Decker, you better add four or five hours to that estimate."

Nearly all of the people who were waiting to get across

came running down and crowded on the bank, staring across at this new catastrophe. Bill heard Benson cursing softly, torridly. On the faces of most of the rest was apathy, resignation. The feeling seemed to be duplicated on the far side of the river, where weary men stood and stared at the beast of a truck on its side in the water.

Chapter Seven

WHEN Linda had heard the grating crack of barrel steel on the skull of her young husband, had seen him turn with a dazed question in his eyes and go down heavily into the roadway, she had forgotten for a time the way his hand had cracked her across the mouth, forgotten his hysteria.

She went to him and turned him over, completely stunned by the casual brutality of the men who had struck him. It was a manner of life completely outside of her experience, and there was enough of the primitive in her so that she did not break down, but instead turned to the nearest possible source of help, the tall, wind-bitten man with the gray eyes, the quietness in his slow voice.

She looked at him in appeal and saw the wariness in his eyes, sensed his reluctance. For a time she thought he might turn away, and then he flipped the cigarette aside, squared his shoulders, and walked toward the armed men.

She knelt by her husband, reached out, groped for his glasses, put them in her purse without for a moment taking her eyes from the tall wedge of Texan back. As John Carter Gerrold sighed, as a child will in its sleep, she saw the aimed blow and cried out, but her cry came after Bill Danton had dodged the blow, came as his heavy hand swiped down and slammed the attacker into the dirt. It all happened with a frightening speed. She caught the wink of murder in the opaque eyes of another, heard the shot, flattened by space and heat, and did not know in that moment if the bullet had hit Bill Danton. She thought it had, and she remembered his reluctance, knew that the moral guilt was hers. And then they grabbed him and ran him against the side of the car, the two stocky men handling him easily, as though he were a long-legged rag doll.

For a time the man who was her husband, sitting up slowly, slack-faced, was forgotten. She saw the acts in the tableau, but she could not understand the words. John stood up, protesting as they took the stretcher gently from the truck. His face looked bald and naked without the glasses, the eyes peering and vague.

They were urged into the second sedan and it followed the first one up the braced planks onto the deck. There was the driver, and one guard, in the car with them. As soon as the wheels were blocked on the ferryboat deck, the driver and guard got out, leaving the three of them alone.

She saw how pale he was. "How do you feel, John?"

He looked at her as though trying to remember who she could be. "All right. How did this happen?"

"Mr. Danton fixed it. He asked the man to do it."

"He did better than I did." John said bitterly. "Everybody goes better than I do. Danton, Benson, that Mooney girl."

"You're doing all you can, John."

"Within the limitations of my ability."

His mother was between them. Now she was a stranger to Linda. She had been a stranger before, also. A compact, merry woman with cool eyes, treating her daughter-in-law as a necessary evil. Treating her not as a person, but as something she disapproved of, yet thought was probably necessary to the well-being of John Carter Gerrold. Like the red bicycle at twelve and the catboat at fourteen and Dartmouth at eighteen. John was the picture, and a toy or a college or a wife were changing frames for the picture. Linda had felt strongly that Mrs. Gerrold had judged her purely on the basis of probable virginity at the time of marriage, and personal cleanliness. There had been the air of "I *do* hope she will amuse John."

But this strangeness was different. She had ceased to be a human, had become an organism that sucked air.

Linda had neither hated nor resented her. In instinctive wiseness, she had merely been biding her time. John could be emotionally weaned, she had thought. There were years to come. Boy-child could become man. And there were more rewards in being married to a man than in having to take over the characteristics of proxy mother. Time was on her side, and proximity would be on her side. Not for a moment had she doubted her eventual victory until, in the store, his blow had stunned her.

The river-bank violence had been an oddly shaped wedge driven into her mind, letting in light where there had been no light before. Linda had thought herself wise in the world's ways. She had successfully fought off her quota of amorous drunks, had competed for a living in a vicious half-world where the gentlest words were like knives for the unwary back. And when things get too rough, call a cop.

But that scene on the river bank had been outside her experience. No cop could be called. There was no last resource, except in yourself. Previously the world had been like the case of the two brave, charming kids, that delightful young couple living so valiently on fifty bucks a week—but with Papa in the background to help out.

Light had entered where before there was no light, and, looking at her young husband across the unconscious body of his mother, she felt that she had come to a moment of decision. She had thought herself a tough little realist. Yet she had made the assumption that John Carter Gerrold was innately fine and brave and decent and tender and honorable. A rather idealized picture. And, with the new light that had entered her mind, she wondered if perhaps, once the mother image had been destroyed, she would find a man who, through selfishness, could become a petty tyrant. Perhaps she had confused weakness with sensitivity.

The ferry moved across the river with all the puffy dignity of a matron crossing against a red light.

She thought, there must be some formula you can use about people, some lens to look through. And suddenly she realized that there was one thing she had never considered. Her young husband had a very curious sense of humor. He could see wryness in the world, and he could enjoy irony, but he was absolutely incapable of laughing at himself, ever. She remembered the night in New York when the handle of the taxi door had devilishly insinuated itself into his trousers pocket and the departing cab had ripped the pocket away, exposing his leg through a great triangular tear. She remembered her instinctive laughter, and the stony look in his eyes that had silenced her at once. The damage to the suit could have meant nothing to him; he could afford a dozen. She remembered that his complaints, until he had gone back to the hotel to change, had been oddly close to whining. And she had excused him for that, on the grounds that to any person just learning to stand on his own feet, personal dignity was a bit too important.

And so the problem could be restated. She could ask herself calmly, Can any person lead a happy life with another person who finds it impossible to laugh at himself?

That problem was less complicated, easier to state than to ask if she could live with a man who, out of fear and petulance, could strike her. She thought of the way they had gone away from the others, to the grove far down the river bank. All that had happened in another existence. It had been another girl who had taken her young husband to that place, who had seduced him—a rather silly girl who had believed at that time that the key to marriage was basically sexual. And the silly girl had wept and taken in her arms an unwilling boy whose honesty in love was forever diluted by a shallowness of spirit.

To all of the young girls of the world, she thought, the white knights come riding. They ride out of the story-page castles and the old line drawings, and from their lances waves milady's scarf. And it is something you have to have so badly that you can take a talkative, easily hurt, mother-dominated, egocentric young man and cloak him in all the silver armor of the questing knight.

On this day she had reached out to her husband and found that the story-page Merlin had said his wry incantation, and the knight was forever gone, and she knew in sudden wisdom that the only way she could ever make a marriage of it was to replace the mother image, until, in a Dali horror, he dangled from her breast. Make him dominate her and he would do so, would learn to do so, and would do it with all the cruelty of the insecure, complaining about her before others, bringing a tyrant gloom into the home.

The clarity of her insight, the irrefutability of her understanding, and the desperation that came from knowing the true extent of the mistake she had made—all shocked her. She knew that she had grown older on this day, and that John Carter Gerrold would never grow older. It made her think of pictures she had seen of a savage tribe where the skulls of infants are encircled by metal bands, so that in adulthood their heads are a shape of horror. Mrs. Gerrold, with the help of her husband's escape, had managed to bind John's emotions so that though the body became a man, the mind remained that of a clever child. Children never laugh at themselves.

They had reached the far shore. The men worked furiously with shovels, and slowly the ferry was hauled closer until the planks could be set in place and blocked. The cars moved down the planks and roared up the winding road onto pavement that led into San Fernando.

"She seems quieter," John said. "God, the way her hands were! I'll never forget it."

"She'll be all right."

"And what do you think you know about it?" he demanded, his voice growing shrill.

She could see him then, as a child, stubbing his toe on a chair, then kicking the chair with all his might, screaming at it. She was something to kick.

"Don't take it out on me," she said softly.

"I think you like all this. I think you hope she dies."

"That isn't worth answering."

He looked at her, and the naked eyes filled with tears. "I . . . I don't know what I'm saying."

They stopped at the public square. The guard smiled and said something in Spanish and made a gesture that said, unmistakably, "Stay right where you are."

He went into the building. He was back soon, with

the doctor. The doctor was a small brown man with hollow cheeks and a lantern jaw. He said. "Please, you get out, I get in."

She got out of the car and stood on the cobblestones and watched through the window as the doctor, cricket-spry, hopped in beside Mrs. Gerrold. He put claw fingers on her pulse, moving his lips as he counted. With his free hand he thumbed up her eyelid, then laid the back of his hand against her forehead.

He stepped out, smiling so gaily that Linda knew at once that the illness was not serious.

Smiling, the doctor said, "Very bad. Seek."

"Is there a hospital heré?" John asked, voice shaking.

The little doctor pointed vaguely toward the second story of the building. "Is hospital. My hospital."

"What's wrong with her?" John asked.

Again he smiled so very gaily. "Have not English. A thing in here." He tapped his forehead. "Very bad."

The guard talked to the doctor in brisk Spanish. The doctor kept smiling and nodding. Linda began to realize that his smile was one of nervousness, not gaiety.

The guards went upstairs and came back down with a canvas stretcher. On the canvas was a great stain, a dark reddish brown. Linda felt her stomach turn over as she realized it was blood.

They set the stretcher on the cobblestones. With the doctor still smiling, giving orders, the men carefully moved the woman out and stretched her out on the stained canvas.

John said, "This is no good, Linda. They must have a phone in this town. I'll get somebody down from Brownsville. A doctor and an ambulance. Why does he keep smiling as if it was all a big joke?"

"Shall I try to phone?"

"You go up with her and I'll see if I can phone. What's the word? *Telefono?*"

"*Teléfono,* I think. There's an accent on it somewhere."

He started off. She saw one of the guards catch his arm and take him over to the lead car, where the toadlike man sat in the back seat. She followed the stretcher up the flight of stone stairs to the office. To her surprise, the office equipment looked gleaming, modern, expensive. Through an open doorway she could see into a small ward where there were four beds. A child was in one, apparently sleeping. The doctor had the men hold the stretcher level beside one of the beds. A pretty pale-skinned nurse came to help. She stripped the bed back and they eased Mrs. Gerrold off the stretcher and into the bed while Linda watched.

The men set the stretcher down, smiled at Linda, spoke to the doctor, and left. The nurse said something to the doctor. He bent over the bed. He came out to Linda, still smiling. "Sorry," he said. "Señora is dead."

The smile made it an obscene joke. Linda brushed past him and stood over the bed. The nurse eyed her gravely. Linda looked down at the damp gray face of the dead woman. There was no doubt.

The doctor appeared at her elbow with a glass. "Dreenk, please," he said, smiling.

She drained the glass mechanically. It was water with something added that gave it a faintly bitter flavor. The doctor took the empty glass.

He said, "Body go to Estados Unidos, yes?"

"Yes."

"Bad heat. Is better ice. Is a man here in San Fernando can fix and take body to Matamoros, yes?"

"My husband will decide."

"Yes."

And she heard his familiar steps on the stone stairs. She turned and met him as he came across the office. He tried to brush by her, saying, "Where is she?"

Linda caught his wrists. "Please, darling. She . . . died, just a minute ago."

He looked at her vacantly. "Eh? What?" He snatched his hands away from her and went to his mother. He flung himself against the edge of the bed, kneeling on the floor, his face against the sheet beside her, one arm flung across her. He cried, vocalizing each sob as children will. His spasms shook her, so that in a horrid moment it seemed to Linda that the dead woman was suppressing laughter that shook her body. The doctor stood smiling. John's sobs began to sound like laughter. She felt the emptiness and dizziness as the room darkened. It was the nurse who saw it. She came quickly to Linda, took her arm, led her into the outer office to a chair, made her sit down, pushed her head forward gently until Linda sat with her head between her knees. Darkness moved back and away from her, and the singing sound left her ears. She straightened up and listened to John weep and knew he was done, finished. He would make no decisions.

She stood up tentatively, and then went to him. "John!"

"Leave . . . me alone!"

"The doctor says there's a man here who can take the body to Matamoros. You have your papers and hers, and you can get her across the border and arrange for the body to be shipped to Rochester. Can you do that? Are you listening?"

"I . . . I'll go with her."

"How about our car? I better go back and get it. Where will I meet you?"

"I don't know."

"Tell the Brownsville police where you register. I'll check with them. Will you do that?"

He didn't turn. "Yes," he said, his voice muffled, mouth against the sheet.

"You gave that girl the car keys?"

"Yes."

"Give me some money."

He took his wallet out of his pants, handed it blindly back to her. She took it, opened it, took out several twenty-peso notes and fifty dollars in United States currency. She put the wallet on the edge of the bed beside his hand. She looked at his hand, then bent over and looked at it more closely, wondering why on earth he should be holding so tightly to a cheap yellow mechanical pencil. She hadn't seen it before, in his pocket.

"Any Brownsville undertaker will ship the body to Rochester."

"Please stop talking to me."

"Maybe in Matamoros you'll have to phone an undertaker to come across the river to get the body."

"I'm not a child. I can do what has to be done."

"Maybe you should come back with me and let the doctor's friend handle it."

"She's dead now. You don't have to be jealous of her any more."

Linda turned and walked out. She went down the stone steps and out onto the narrow sidewalk. It was perceptibly cooler, and the buildings on the west side of the square cast shadows that touched the bases of the buildings on the opposite side. The black sedan had gone. From a corner cantina came the thin strains of a guitar, a nasal tenor singing *"María Bonita."* A pup trotted sideways down the middle of the street. A ragged child appeared from nowhere, saying, *"Un centavo, señorita, un centavo, por favor."*

She turned toward the river. The child followed.

She felt insulated from all the world, as though she walked inside an invisible capsule through which all sound and vision came dimly. She guessed that it was the result of whatever the doctor had given her. It seemed good to be walking, and to be alone. Two young men leaned against the outside wall of a pink building. They followed her with their eyes. When she was ten paces beyond them, she heard the low whistle, *whee-whew,* the favor that all Mexican males seemed to feel obligated to award to any pale-haired girl.

It no longer seemed important to think of her marriage as a dilemma. She would go on with John, or she wouldn't. She had been tricked. She had given her body to the white knight who had never been. Given it with a high eagerness.

The sidewalk ended and the wide shoulder of the road was hard-baked, pebbled. The chanting child gave up the pursuit. She passed a gas station, a soft-drink stand. She wished that she would never reach the river, would merely walk on through this dusking day. Women passed her balancing vast bundles of cotton clothing on their heads—clothing that had been washed in the mud of the river, dried and bleached in the sun.

The road circled down the edge of the river bank, and as she came around the turn she saw the truck on its side, oddly helpless, like a horse that has fallen on the ice. Men squatted in the water, grunting and sweating over jacks and blocks. There seemed no organization in their efforts, no one to direct the operation. Only four cars waited on this side of the river. Looking across, she saw that the road on the far side was now entirely in shadow, the sun having sunk low enough to be cut off by the crest of the hill, and soon this bank, too, would be in shadow. She could see that the MG and the pickup still headed the line and knew that this truck must have fallen from the planks into the river soon after the two black sedans had disembarked.

She stood a long time, placidly, just watching them. She was in no haste to make a decision of any kind. The effects of the sedative still clung, like cotton, to the fringes of her mind, and it was almost with a sense of loss that she felt the effect diminishing, fading, her head clearing.

A gnarled boatman came grinning up to her, gesturing, pointing to her, pointing across the river, pointing down to a flat-bottomed scow. He kept holding up three fingers, saying, "Solamente tres pesos, señorita."

She stared at him blankly for a time, and then nodded and followed him down to his boat. He steadied it as she got in. She sat on the middle seat as he directed, the skirt of the tan linen dress tucked around her knees. He sat in the stern and sculled it across with a single oar, keeping the blunt bow pointed upstream, so that the boat, angling across, made her think of the pup who had trotted down the middle of the San Fernando street.

Bill Danton left the group he was with and sauntered down to meet her, his thumbs tucked under the belt of the khaki work pants. He pulled the bow up, gave her his hand, and helped her out. She turned and handed the boatman his fee. He bobbed his head and grinned.

"What happened?" Bill Danton asked.

"She . . . died. Just as we got her up to the doctor's and got her into bed she . . ."

And without clearly knowing the reason, she found that she was crying. And it was not the death, not that loss. It was another loss, a different thing entirely, that had been taken from her on this day, leaving her with an emptiness beyond description and beyond belief. And his arm was surprisingly light around her shoulders, and the soothing sounds he made only made the tears come faster.

Chapter Eight

FOR Darby Garon, the middle-aged adulterer, there was the torment of the sun, and the greater torment of remorse and self-disgust.

Moira was a crisp green island on a far horizon. He could see the far island while he strangled in a warm sea of smothering breast and massive clasping flank. Through the long hours of afternoon he sat alone and wondered how this thing, this so trite and ordinary thing, had happened to him.

All his life he had enjoyed crisp, clean, delicate things. As a boy he had collected butterflies, mint postage stamps, fossil rocks. His father had helped him build the display cases.

He had been a quiet, introverted boy, but with a tough streak of ambition that had brought him eventual success. He had made few friends, but those few were good friends, lasting friends.

During the afternoon he noticed the illness of the gray-haired woman, Betty's new friendship with the stocky hard-faced man, the arrival of the blonde twins. He noted them, but they were not important. They were figures moving around in an unreal world. The realities were inside of him, and he knew that if he were ever able to live again with himself without shame, he would have to understand what had motivated this crazy escapade that could have already lost him home, wife, and position.

Clean things he had always loved. Piano fugues. The scent of pine. And when the kids were younger, the look of the way the hair curled at the napes of fragile necks, the sleepy warm scent of them.

In college there had been a cursory examination of philosophy, of psychology, and through those courses he had gained a necessary bit of self-knowledge. He had learned that each man has black and evil thoughts, and that those thoughts are not a proof of variance, but rather a proof of kinship with the rest of men. The mind forever contains lust and malice and hate, and when you can keep those instincts in their proper compartment, then you have become a reasoning animal, a man. Let them escape and you live on the instinctual level of a beast. But there is no shame in owning such instincts—only shame in giving them dominance.

How had this episode come to pass?

How had a hunger arisen that could be sated only by such a one as the full-bodied wench he had picked up on a city street?

Either it was a desire for self-abasement, something born of guilt, or else it was a real hunger, a genuine need.

Had life been sterile and unsatisfying? He knew that it had not. He was ambitious, and he had satisfied the full extent of his ambitions with a job paying forty thousand a year. He knew that he had the mental equipment to have gone higher, and yet did not because his ambition lacked that final edge of ruthlessness.

The kids were good. Basically good. They had made their full share of problems, yet in the home there had been enough love, enough security, so that they faced the world with that assurance which is real, rather than the false boldness that is the result of overprotection.

The key would have to be Moira. The answer would have to lie within his relationship to Moira. He could still remember how she was when he had first seen her on the campus. Not a tall girl, but, because of the clean good bones, looking taller than she was. Brown hair and the serious mouth and the eyes that were bottomless. Heavy stack of books in her arm.

In a first afternoon, during a first walk, talk had skipped rapidly from inconsequentialities to the larger matters of life and death, which were also, perhaps, inconsequentialities of another degree.

Both of them had come from rigidly conservative New England homes. They fought together behind the barri-

cades of the radical outlook, and both of them were in
healthy revolt against their very similar background.

In a week they knew they were in love. They said a
million words to each other and knew they were in love.
But this, of course, was a love that transcended all stuffy
middle-class conventions. Love like this could only be
stultified by ageless words said over them, by a slip of
paper from the state that was merely official permission
to sleep with each other. Should a child come of such a
union, they could raise the child in an atmosphere of
moral freedom and intellectual honesty that had been
denied them. It was only due to their quite exceptional
intelligences that, of course, they had seen through the
constricting bonds on their immortal souls and had de-
clared their freedom.

Sitting there in the shade, he almost smiled as he remembered the clumsiness.

In the first place, it had been very difficult to arrange.
They managed to fix it for Easter vacation. A fraternity
brother of his promised to protect him on a fictitious
vacation visit to the brother's home in Hartford, and
then made comments so lewd that Darby came within an
inch of slugging him and spoiling it all. And Moira had
made a similar arrangement with a good friend of hers.

In the kitty was an unspent Christmas fifty dollars from
an aunt of Moira's, and a hundred dollars taken by
Darby with great guile from his own savings account.

On the train down to New York Moira had been hecti-
cally gay, flushed cheeks hiding what he learned later to
be pure fear. And he remembered how the excitement
came leaping into his throat each time he looked at her
sitting beside him.

Together they had found a small cheap hotel in the
Village, with the lobby on the second floor. A lobby full
of jowled men reading papers and scratch sheets.

"Mr. and Mrs. D. C. Garon," he had written in the
register, having explained to her that such a fiction
would be necessary, and though they could be contemptu-
ous of such a formalized relationship, hotel people could
not be expected to understand the newer freedom.

Their room contained a vast double bed, a truly stupendous and overpowering and embarrassingly beddy
bed, the essence of all beds. The exact center of it was a
good six inches lower than the surrounding edges. When
they were left alone in the shoddy room, left with their
two suitcases, the bed dominated the room and dominated them. It was a bed that made you want to tiptoe and
speak in whispers. The single window looked out over
a tarry roof littered with papers, and so one could not
pretend to admire a view. They stood at the window,
stood a careful foot apart, and were dominated by the
bed of all beds.

And he had cleared his throat and said, "Moira, dearest, I think we should prove to ourselves that we didn't
come here . . . just to . . . just to . . ."

She turned shining eyes on him. "Of course! We'll
prove that we're above the . . . the needs of the flesh."

He was obscurely irritated by the eagerness with which
she had grabbed at the straw. "For tonight, at least," he
said, a bit grumpily.

"Yes, my darling."

And they had found a candlelight restaurant and some
cheap red wine, and drowned mightily in each other's eyes
and gone back to the shadow of the imperious bed. It
had been a difficult matter to arrange. In the end he had
taken his suitcase down the hall to the bathroom, changed
there into pajamas and robe, repacked his clothes, and,
after giving her more than enough time, had trudged
back to the room.

She lay, looking oddly small, on the far edge of the
huge bed. He had turned out the light, put his robe
aside, slipped in on his side.

"You could anyway kiss me good night, dearest," she
whispered.

They had met in the hollow of the great bed, his arms
around her, hands on silk with warmth that came sleek
through the silk. He kissed her and, holding her thus,
realized with a sudden horror that despite all his serious
attempts at spirituality the rebellious body was going to
announce its presence in an unmistakable way. And so

he had stabbed her lips with a hasty kiss, muttered a gruff good night, and clawed his way up the slope to his brink of the bed. And in the morning they had awakened, mashed together in the deep slope of the bed, and again he had escaped in time.

On the next night they had brought a bottle of red, red wine to the room, and he had managed to act extremely dense each time she made an indirect plea for the continuance of their task of proving that the flesh was subordinate.

He was not prepared, he remembered, for the task at hand. The rumble seats of roadsters and the roadside blankets and the few expert practitioners he had encountered had given him a false sense of his own abilities.

So she had gone all atremble and kept whispering, "No!" even while her arms clung to him, and at last there was a shriek, thin as bat sound, and the sobs, the brokenhearted flat sobbings, and the accusations and a quarrel that went on until, with dawn like a milk spray on the window, she had fallen into exhausted sleep in his arms.

He knew that it could have ended there, with no fulfillment for either of them, but they were proud and they were stubborn, and she later found it possible to see if the damn thing could be done or if there was something wrong with her. And, remembering the way he had looked down at her pale stoic face, remembering the way she had said, "No, don't stop. I might as well find out right now," he relived that day and wanted to cry as he remembered.

For then, as all was lost, her face changed and her body changed and she shifted a bit and they were lost in each other, and found a new crazy world all their own. They got drunk on that world and overstayed until she had to go back on a coach while he hitchhiked.

And two months later they were married, telling each other that their parents, though deluded, were really old sweeties, and after all it was just a gesture, and they could live together just as freely, state permission or no state permission.

No, there had been nothing wrong with their love.

Her arms, over the years, had been what he had wanted them to be. The children were love children. And Moira had never lost that clean-lined look or her almost maidenly modesty.

They shared friends and books and records. They had towering quarrels and made up, and were closer for having quarreled. And during the past five years they had reached that point of mutual understanding where little has to be said with words.

When should he have become aware that this Mexican escapade was a possibility?

He remembered the puzzled face of a secretary he had fired. He had been unable to give her a good reason, and, out of guilt, had found her a job that paid just a bit more than he was paying her. The firing had been precautionary, because he had found just a bit too much pleasure at looking at the ripe line of her flank, at the heavy curve of breast, and he had found himself wondering vaguely how he could arrange to give her overtime work so that they would be in the office together at night. And so he had fired her. That had been a clue, a warning.

And he remembered the way the young girls had begun to look. They had changed somehow. Become more provocative. Loneliness and restlessness and an inexplicable hunger.

Betty Mooney had fed that hunger.

He flushed as he remembered the days and the nights with her. Never, even in the early days with Moira, had he been so blindingly sensual, so unremittant in his demands, so goatily persistent. It was as though sex were a candle that had burned with a steady flame through the years, and now, reaching the end, the wick flared up and guttered and burned twice as brightly during those last moments before flickering out entirely.

It seemed almost as though, in sating this last hunger, he had consciously sought someone as unlike Moira as possible.

Betty Mooney was flabby nightmare. And Moira would detect the sick scent of her on his soul. He did not know what it might do for Moira, for such an intensely loyal woman. He knew that any infidelity on her part was in-conceivable.

The image of the sick woman being carried out to the truck flickered across his brain, leaving no residue. He had seen Betty with the tough-faced man several times during the afternoon. He hoped she would go away with him, take her loot out of the car and get out of his life. He looked to be her sort. Shrewd, ignorant, acquisitive.

Moments later, two black sedans went by at a reckless speed, roiling up the dust, passing all the other cars in line. The dust made him cough. He leaned more heavily against the tree, wondering what on earth he could say to Moira. Their relationship was irretrievably lost, gone forever.

Far down the road there was some kind of scuffle, a man falling down in the dust, the pale-haired girl going to him. And then another man and a scuffle and some-one falling.

Suddenly his attention was ripped away from the distant scene when one of the children playing in the road hit him in the belly with a stone hurled so hard that it felt like a blow from a hammer.

He glared around. The children were not playing any more. Some of them had drifted down the road. Others had been called back by their parents. Damn fools who couldn't teach their children a little common considera-tion. The blow had given him an oddly hollow feeling.

Suddenly he felt a warm wetness, a stickiness around his groin. He opened his shirt and looked at where the stone had hit him. There was a small hole, and blood ran slowly out of the hole and down under his belt.

And he knew that there had been a shot and he said, aloud, "I'm shot!" It sounded like a remarkably stupid and self-evident thing to say. And he was filled with sur-prise rather than panic. Gangsters get shot. Soldiers get shot. Darby Garon, executive, does not get shot. But there was the hole, with little raw edges, and one cannot very well refute the evidence of a hole in one's own belly. The shot, a wild one, had apparently come out of that scuffle down there by the river bank.

One must be logical in all things. If one has a bullet hole in one, it is well to have it tended to. He remembered what he had read about being shot in the belly. In Civil War days it was invariably fatal. In World War I days, it had been damn serious. But now, with sulpha and penicillin and so on, it was just an abdominal operation, with the perforated intestines sewed up, and a handful or two of magic powder tossed in the incision, and a month of bed rest.

A sudden cramp pulled his lips back from his teeth. He shook his head. It felt just like a bad case of gas. Suddenly the Mexican escapade diminished in importance, and Betty Mooney was not someone to hate. She was someone to help him. He looked around and saw her, far down the road.

Might as well wait until I feel a little stronger, he thought, and then get close enough to yell to her. Said she did some nursing work once upon a time. She'll know how to handle this.

The second cramp was worse than the first. It banged his knees up against his chest. He slowly forced them down again, taking a deep breath, closing his eyes for a bit. Panic began to stir around in the back of his mind. He forced it aside. Hell, you could live for days with a hole in your belly. Or could you? Didn't it have to miss important organs? He squinted down at the river bank and then looked at the hole again. He carefully pulled his shirt back over the hole, tucked it in gently. He wedged his hand under his belt so that the heel of his right thumb was pressed hard against the wound. It made it feel a little better. When he didn't look at it, it felt as big as a dinner plate. He had to keep remembering the size of it, the exact size. Now, with a slug coming from that angle, where would it be? He used his left hand to feel around in back of himself. He felt no stickiness. So the thing was still in there. A little lead pellet. He remembered buying the older boy a .22, and how they had plinked at tin cans out near the woods. You had to keep telling a kid that those little things can kill a man, or a boy.

Maybe it could lodge in a kidney or something. What would that do? Live for days. Just a case of getting attention.

A man walked by. Darby started to call to him, but just as he opened his mouth the third cramp tortured him. He felt as though a big hand was grabbing his guts and twisting hard, holding tight, then slowly letting go. When he opened his eyes again and got his knees down, the man was gone.

Damn silly situation. Make you feel a little stupid and helpless. Goddamn that girl! Why didn't she come up and see how things were going? Be a hell of a joke on her if he died. Nice job explaining it. Executive goes on marital vacation. Dies on river bank in Mexico. Mistress implicated. Says she was not anywhere near Garon at time of death.

Stop thinking that way. There's a lot in this thinking business. Think of something long enough and hard enough and it happens to you. Every time. Like wanting that dream house. Moira got it, too, finally. Lot of work, lot of years. But she got it.

Panic grew stronger and, with rat teeth, made lace of the edge of his mind. He got his feet under him, craned his left hand back, and braced it against the trunk of the tree. Now, one little push, Darby, and you'll be on your feet. Then you can walk forty paces. Hell, you've been walking all your life. No trick to it. Just one foot in front of the other.

He shoved mightily and rocked onto his feet, doubled over. He felt curiously weak. The strength didn't run out of a man that fast. A cramp hit him before he could take a step. The cramp pressed his buttocks down against his heels and he rocked back, the tree striking him in the back again. The world tilted and slowly regained an even keel. The cramp faded, but this time it didn't go away entirely.

Take a little rest and then another try. This is a lot of silliness. More guts than this in the Garon clan. Remember Uncle Ralph? Chopped right through his boot and severed three toes and walked home. Nine miles, they said it was. Home with a grin and a white face and a boot full of blood, falling face down in the kitchen.

And, waiting for the strength to try again, he knew sourly that he was going to die. The panic of a few minutes before had faded utterly. Dying was now a damn inconvenience. Bonds in bad shape. Never changed the insurance options like Harry suggested. Damn little in the checking account, too. Moira would have to get a loan until the insurance was paid off. Harry would fix it for her, but she wouldn't like having to ask. Maybe he'd have sense enough to offer it to her.

What are you talking about, man? There are a lot of years left. A lot of suns coming up. Grandchildren to spoil. And that trip to take, the trip Moira wants. Acapulco, Rio. Trip you've been saving for, as much as taxes will let you.

Got to get the car back, drive that bitch to San Antone. Or did she come from Houston? Hard to remember which. So you had a merry three-week roll in the hay, and now you're shot in the belly, and a very just little punishment it is. If that hole had been four inches lower, it would have been an even juster punishment. It would have done a good job on the equipment that got you into this jam. If thine eye offend thee . . .

His chin was on his chest. He lifted it with great effort. The scene wavered a bit and then came clear. Startlingly clear. He could see the muddy river, the far shore. Ferry was on the other side. The black cars going up the road. And a small figure over there . . .

Hell, what had been the matter with his eyes! Even at that distance, you could tell the brown hair, and that sweater and skirt. Bought that outfit for her for her birthday. God, that was a long time ago. Thought she'd worn it out and thrown it away, long ago. One thing about Moira. She always used her head. One sharp girl. Traced him somehow. Came riding, riding, riding up to the old inn door. No, wrong line. Came riding to the rescue.

He grinned at the figure of his wife on the far shore. Now everything was fine. Sure, even at that distance he could read her eyes. He could read the sweet forgiveness, and the understanding. She knew the answers. She'd tell him why he'd done this thing to the two of them, and he would understand when she had told him.

The sweet kid, she was standing over there with books held tightly in her arm, just like during campus days.

That was her way of showing him that everything was all right. A nice symbol. A nice gesture.

He got easily and quickly to his feet, bounded down through the ditch, and went swinging down the road, his head high.

She saw him, and she lifted her free arm and waved. And he broke into a run. Hadn't run for years. Thought I'd forgotten how. But look at me go! Just like the coach said. Knees high and a lot of spring in the foot and stay up on your toes, Garon.

Running, running, with the wind in his face, running by all the surprised people who thought he was too old and too tired to run. And the river bank was speeding toward him, the way you'd see it from the windshield of a fast car. And Darby Garon went out in a flat dive, hitting the water, knifing down through the water, down through the blackness, feeling it against his face, like dark wings, knowing that he would rise to the surface and she would be close, and there would never again be any problems between them. With his arms straight out in front of him, and with a smile on his lips, he knifed through the blackness, waiting forever for the moment when he would begin to rise toward the surface.

Chapter Nine

Riki, unaccompanied by her twin blonde sister, walked slowly up the road to the car. Funny kind of dusk they had here. Not like the ones they used to have in Ohio when she was a child. Here it was all yellow, glaring, one minute, and then—poom!—purple like the dresses Granny used to wear for best, and the stars began to show on the eastern horizon almost before the sun was down.

She got into the Packard, unlatched the top, pushed the button. The top went up and then slid slowly down into the well with an asthmatic whining. She climbed into the back and lit a cigarette. The tequila glow had faded to a bad taste in her mouth. She considered refurbishing the glow from one of the unopened bottles and then gave it up.

Riki and Niki. Even the names were cheap and phony. How dumb could you get?

What did Granny use to say? Would some power the giftie gie us . . .

Well, that guy from New York had really pulled the rug from under them.

Been a lot better if they'd gone right on from high school, even if it meant waiting on tables. Northwestern was handy.

Sooner or later they were going to have to tell Phil. A sweetie. Anxious little guy, sweating and fuming and working, with that big dream ahead of him, the dream he'd got too old for.

Gee, she thought, after we saw how that duet strip went over in New Orleans, we thought we really had something. It seemed kinda cute, damnit. Phil had worked it up. Just a simple backdrop with a doorway cut in it, and the doorway was supposed to be a mirror. They'd practiced making the same moves so that people said it really did look like a mirror. And there was a dressing table over at the side. They took turns being the girl behind the mirror. With the music going, you just sat at the dressing table and put on one of the hats and tilted it right, and then went over and looked at yourself in the full-length mirror. The girl on the other side was dressed the same as you. And with the second hat, they began to get the idea, when they saw that the mirror image was wearing fewer clothes each time, even though the girl in front didn't take a thing off. Gee, they'd hollered and stomped enough in New Orleans, and in Mexico too. The first few times were tough, all right, because you kept thinking how Granny would have whaled the tar out of you if she'd seen what you were doing.

But Phil said a little strip kept the act alive, and you got good practice out of the rest of the routines. And so you got sort of accustomed to showing yourself off, and it helped to know that there was something to show.

God, how we used to talk it over when we were little kids. Little Mary Anne and Ruthie Sheppard, yaking to all hours of the night in that big bed, about how we were going to be an act. Singing and dancing. The Sheppard Sisters. Learning all the popular songs.

The big night was winning that amateur thing. And having the man sign us up to compete against the winners of the other amateur things. And when little Phil turned up with his sarcasm, and telling us we didn't know a damn thing yet, and he could help us, gee, how we jumped at it!

He made us work, all right, and he's a nice guy, and he means well, and how could he possibly know that he was teaching us all the wrong things?

That guy from New York, he fixed us good, him and his fancy friends. They caught the show, a whole tableful of them, and when he sent the note back for us to join their party, just the two of us, not Phil, Phil read the note and his eyes went real wide open and he said, "Jimmy Angus! Say, I heard of him. Mixed up in musicals in New York. A big shot. Look, gals, be on your best behavior. This could be a break."

So we went to the table and there's that trick we used since we were kids, of Mary Anne starting sentences and me finishing them without a break. Funny now to think of her as Mary Anne instead of Niki.

Well, it seemed to go over pretty good, and we worked in some of the gags that we learned from Phil, and they all laughed like crazy, and maybe we should have known because there was a funny little edge in all the laughing. They weren't really with us.

Jimmy Angus was a big skinny guy, sort of old, and the girl with the boy's haircut was his wife and she used to be an actress, and then there was a fat agent from Hollywood, and the redhead, and some young guy with an old bag of a wife, and some spare people.

It's hard to figure out now whether it was a mistake to go to the hotel suite with them all or not. Maybe we'd have been better off to go ahead being dumb. It certainly was one hell of a big layout there in the Del Prado. Biggest hotel suite I ever saw. With a bartender from the hotel all set up in a little alcove, and more people coming in, and we finally got the drift that they were all down there figuring out some kind of angle on doing a Mexican movie. It was pretty hard to follow a lot of the conversation. We stuck close together, as usual.

We thought we were sort of like friends, and for a while there it was kind of exciting, because they certainly all acted famous, even though we hadn't heard of any of them.

Phil had told us to be on our best behavior, so we did a lot of drink-nursing. I didn't get the drift at all when Jimmy Angus started arranging a table, but then when he came out with an armload of hats and dumped them on the table, it began to worry me.

He banged on a glass, like at a banquet for the speaker, and he said, "And now for your pleasure, Angus and Company present the show-stopper from the Club de Medianoche—Riki and Niki and their very obvious talents. Let's go, gals." He trotted over to one of those little pianos and began the theme we use for the act, "Lovely to Look At."

We looked at each other, and we always seem to think alike and get the same reaction to things, and I knew we'd both fallen flat down with a big thud. We'd thought we were guests, and now we were supposed to strip for this crazy drunk crowd. It was tough enough to do it in a club, but in a club it was sort of impersonal; we weren't going to undress in anybody's living room, that was for sure.

"No." I said. "No, please."

The fat agent came over and gave us a sort of greasy smile and he handed us a fifty-dollar bill each and said, "For that, ladies, I think you can go on with the act, without making that little concession to censorship like you do at the club."

By the time I'd figured out what he was saying to us, that he expected us to go through with it completely starko, he'd eased back away from us, and there we were with our bare faces hanging out and the fifties in our hand, and everybody looking, and that Jimmy Angus, grinning over his shoulder at us from the piano bench, still doing our theme. We said no again and they kept applauding and stamping their feet and some jerk was yelling, "Take it off! Take it off!"

And we tried to head toward the door, and some guy came trotting over, a little bitty guy, and he said in a big loud voice that stopped the music, "These little girls are shy, folks." Little girls! He came up to my chin.

He went on and said, "What they need is a little rehearsal. Louie, I'll reimburse you for the hundred bucks, and these little lovelies and I, why, we will retire to a private chamber and get in some practice."

Another guy elbowed in and said, "And by God, for another hundred they'll practice with me, too." All the women yelped like they were shocked or something. The little guy was wiry, and he tried to steer us down toward a sort of hallway.

Mary Anne and I have always worked pretty well together on wise guys. It's something we worked out as far back as eighth grade. She spun him and I hit him, and while he was still spinning she hit him as he came around, and she was crying, and it knocked out a funny little bridge and he fell down and Mary Anne kicked him in the chest. We were both crying then, and it stopped all the noise so you couldn't hear a thing except the little bitty guy saying bad words and crawling toward that little bridge.

We got out the door and Jimmy Angus caught us at the elevator. He had a different look on his face. He said, "I want to talk to you girls."

"And you can go to hell," Mary Anne said, with sobs in her voice like broken springs in a bed.

"I want to tell you something for your own good."

I told him I wouldn't go back in there with those crumbs for a thousand bucks. He told us we didn't have to, and he was very persuasive and he got us down the hall somehow and into a small bedroom. We sat side by side on the bed. He leaned on the bureau with his arms crossed and a cigarette bobbing in the corner of his mouth as he talked. He said, "I'm not going to apologize for what I did. I was misled. Where do you girls come from?"

We didn't want to talk, but he got it out of us, a little bit at a time, until we were interrupting each other to tell him the whole thing. He kept nodding.

Neither of us will ever forget what came next. He took a long time butting his cigarette. He was frowning. "So O.K. So you're a couple of good-looking girls from Ohio. Young and healthy and good. I could kid you along. But I owe you something for what happened in there. That Decker. He's taken a couple of nice kids and turned them into a fair imitation of brass blondes. He's taught you to talk and walk and act like a pair of high-priced whores. He's turned you into a pair of burlesque types. A lot of fine comics have come up from burlesque. They came up because they had sense enough to change their styles and grow. Decker will never be anything but one of the less clever baggy-pants boys. I imagine you girls want to stay in show business. I say, get out. Your voices are true, but too small. Neither of you has the instinctive grace of born dancers. Your only stock in trade is a pair of beautiful bodies and a blue routine. You've had your kicks playing joints with Decker. Go home and get married and have beautiful babies. Now don't interrupt. You can go on with Decker, and I'll tell you exactly what will happen. You'll play joints until your voices sound like whisky tenors. You'll go on and on until you start to sag, and by then Decker will be through, and all you'll have left is heartbreak. And don't be too rough and too indignant when people figure you're both pushovers. Decker has taught you to look like a pair of pushovers. We got you up here for laughs. So we didn't get any laughs, and maybe you made us feel a little ashamed."

He took out a card and scribbled on it and tossed it into Mary Anne's lap. "If you're too stubborn to take good advice, the least you can do is ditch that crumby little comic. Go to the address on that card. He's a friend of mine. He'll place you somewhere in New York after he cures you both of the phony tricks Decker's taught you. Maybe some big club where all you have to do is wear fancy costumes and walk around for the baldies to lick their chops at."

On the way back in the cab we told each other that Jimmy Angus didn't know sugar from Shinola. We were whistling as we walked past our personal cemetery. Angus had shown us the cemetery. With one stone saying Niki and one saying Riki.

Phil was waiting up, all excited about what had happened. We told him that Jimmy Angus had told us to give him a ring in New York. You'd think somebody had just told Phil he'd won a raffle.

The next day we tried to talk Phil into taking the strip out of the routine. It was as easy as taking away his left arm.

What Angus had said worked on us. We talked it over. Niki put it in words finally. She said, "Face it, Buster. Angus gave it to us straight. He opened the window and some fresh air blew in. But can you tell Phil? Can you?"

We knew how much he was counting on us. And we knew the dream. It would have killed the little guy. He was thinking that now he could get into the big time be-

fore it was too late for him. We heard the lines with new
ears, and watched each other with new eyes, and we began
to feel cheap and ashamed and tricked. The life went out
of the act, and the applause lost its edge, but Phil didn't
seem to notice. And the same way we've always done
everything together, we seemed to find out at the same
time that a wee dollop can make the world right rosy and
make you forget that a big suite full of smart show people
thought you were a flooze pair because that's what you
had been taught to act like.

Riki lit another cigarette. The decision had been made.
They had decided to ride along with Phil Decker because
they knew they couldn't hurt him that badly. And, she
thought, it would have been O.K. if they'd been able to
keep moving. You keep moving and you can stop thinking. But get a big fat delay like here at the ferry and you
start turning it over and over in your mind again. The
card Angus had written on was carefully tucked away.
Ugly little man with sparrow legs in those absurd red
shorts. Ugly little man with his tired jokes and his big
dream. What would happen to him? But, on the other
hand, who were they to toss themselves away for the sake
of his impossible dream? She took a hard drag on the
cigarette. Get to New York and then make the break? No,
if any break was going to be made, it ought to be here and
now, here in the protecting darkness of the night.

Niki appeared out of the darkness and leaned against
the side of the car. Her voice was dull. "Sitting this one
out, baby?"

"Sitting and thinking."

"Keep it up. You might have beginner's luck."

"That's Phil's line."

"They're all Phil's lines, baby."

"Mary Anne, I . . ."

"I know, Ruthie. I've been thrashing around the same
way. There's a long life ahead. Sure, he's a sweetie."

"Can we do it?"

"It's dark now. That seems to help a little. Think how
blissfully happy we'd be, baby, if we'd never met one
James Angus. Right now, it all seems kind of nightmarey.

Right now I can't believe I've bared my fair white body for the public. Can you imagine what Granny would say?"

"Be a busy woodshed."

"And food standing up."

"I'm laughing and I feel like crying."

"You know, he's uneasy. He's sensed something wrong. He's a little worried."

"How about a jolt? Will that help?"

"Let's not. It may make us so sentimental, we'll drop the whole thing."

"How are we going to say it?"

"Open up the subject and let the words come."

Instinctively they reached for each other's hands, held tight.

"Agreed?" Riki asked softly.

"O.K. We do it. Sit tight. He'll be hunting us soon."

Niki joined her sister in the back seat of the car. They sat together and there was no need for any more words. In ten minutes Phil Decker came wandering up the road.

"Hey, there you are!" he said, peering into the car. "I think I got a skit figured. We put Niki in a tight skirt leaning on a prop lamppost, see, smoking and swinging a red pocketbook and looking at her watch and stamping her foot to show she's waiting for some guy who's late. I walk by her and turn about and give her the old double take, and then come back casual-like, see. Then—"

"We want to talk to you, Phil," Riki said in a low voice.

"Eh? Don't you want to hear the skit? It's tricky. See, Niki is waiting for a streetcar, but we get the yuk out of it being a streetcar named desire, and the little guy, that's me, gets it wrong and thinks that she . . ."

"We want to say something to you, Phil," Niki interrupted. "So why don't you get in the front seat and turn around and listen?"

"Something wrong? Hell, don't worry about the ferry. We'll get across sometime tonight." He got in the car, turned to face them.

"It's more than that, Phil," Riki said. "Honestly, we're terribly grateful for everything you've done for us."

"But," said Niki, "we want to split."

The silence was heavy. Phil slowly took out a cigarette, lighted it. He let the flame burn for a few seconds before he snapped the lighter shut on it.

"You maybe think that's simple or something?" he said in a harsh voice. "You maybe think you snap your fingers and we're all done? I knew something's been eating on you two. I've had my hunches. Well, let me tell you something. Without old Phil keeping you in shape, you two will be finished in a month."

"We'll take that chance," Riki said, glad that he had taken that attitude.

"You might, and then again you might not," Phil said coldly.

"How do you mean that?"

"It's pretty tough to fool old Phil. I caught that Angus angle. He figures he can use you. Use you is right. He won't do you any good. You can bet on that. Hell, I could see it all shaping up."

"We've talked it over, Phil," Riki said. "And we want to break it up."

"There's a hell of a distance between wanting to and doing it. Don't forget that. I got your names on a little piece of paper. Maybe it don't seem like much to you, that little piece of paper, but let me tell you it's protection. There's no way you can sneak out of it, believe me."

"We talked that over a couple of weeks ago, Phil. We got to appear with you, O.K. But Lincoln stopped slavery. We'll stand there, and you can make all the jokes you want, and it still goes as a fifty-fifty split."

"I'll wait you out, then. We won't work at all."

"We'll work, Phil. We'll wait tables. How long can you wait?"

He suddenly tilted back his head and laughed harshly. "What the hell am I yaking about? Hell, I'm making it sound as if I need you. I need you two like I need a point on my head. I've been doing you a favor. Phil, the softie. Well, it goes to show you. You can't take a couple of farm kids and make show business out of them. I thought I could. So I was wrong. Now I'll give it to you. You got no talent. Neither of you. People beat their hands together

on account of my jokes and on account of you're both
stacked, which is something you were born with. I'm going to pick myself up some real pro gals. A pair that know
the score. Any time you want to come crawling back, write
me care of Variety and I won't answer the letter. You can
mail it in a hole in the ground and get the same answer.
We'll drive to Brownsville and split the kitty and you can
take your clothes. The costumes belong to me, don't forget. And you can take that contract which I am going to
hand to you, and you can pin it on the wall where you can
look at it in the middle of the night when a mess of
squalling brats wake you up, because, gals, without me,
you're just going no place at all in the entertainment business. I've been a sucker, but it's no skin off. You give me
some laughs to remember, and, gals, this is the biggest
laugh of all."

He slammed the car door and went down the road. His
walk was jaunty and he was whistling one of Berlin's
oldies as he walked away.

"The poor little guy," Riki said softly. "Maybe we
ought to give him a year. One more year."

"No, baby. We said it. We did it. We'd never have the
guts to do it twice. Leave it lay."

"But he's such a sweet little old picked chicken."

"Sweet and dumb and hopeless, Riki. Ruthie, I mean.
Riki and Niki are dead."

"The Sheppard twins it is."

"What will happen to him, baby?"

"Who knows? Beer joints. My guess is he'll pick up
some poor kid and make a stripper out of her and ride on
that as far as he can. And maybe she'll never meet a
Jimmy Angus. Did you know the little guy was so proud,
Ruthie?"

"We shot him right through the heart. Proud of us?"

"I don't know yet. Wait till I stop bleeding."

"A knock?"

"I'm off the stuff. Did you see him strut away?"

"A picture to go in my locket."

"Did you ever hear the one about the midget and the
locket?"

"That one is Phil's."

"Own up, Sis. For the rest of our lives we'll probably be using his lines."

"And remembering the little ferry that couldn't."

"Getting a little maudlin, ain't we?"

"Turn your head. I'm going to cry, just a little."

"Maybe you better wait until I'm through."

They sat in the dark car and put their long legs up on the top of the front seat. The night air was soft.

After a long time, Mary Anne began a song, softly, sweetly. Ruthie joined in on the second bar. One of the first songs they had learned.

Their voices were like silver in the night. "I love to tell the story. 'Twill be my theme in glory to tell the old, old story . . ."

And, fifty yards and nearly thirty years away, Phil Decker heard the sweetness, and he hit his thigh with his fist, again and again.

Chapter Ten

Del Bennicke, the tough, stocky fugitive who was calling himself Benson now, counted up and realized he had gone thirty-two hours without sleep. He began to have a somewhat clinical attitude toward himself. It was like being in that stage of drunkenness when you cannot be absolutely certain that you are making sense to others. Fear kept him sleepless, kept him walking on the ends of his nerves, and exhaustion kept him from planning adequately or properly, kept him also from worrying about the quality of his planning.

Somehow, it was going to come out all right. It always had. One minute he would think that. The next instant he would be sweating. One moment he would feel tiredness dragging him down, and then adrenalin would steam through his blood stream, compacting his shoulders, balling his fists, making it hard to take a deep breath.

You used people to get you out of jams. Be fast enough and you could foul up the situation so good you were lost in the crowd.

That little fracas with the guards of the fat politico had set him up, somehow. Made him feel better. The fool kid had practically whammed the gun barrel with the back of his head. The half-spick Texan had done pretty well. Nice dodging, nice backhand slam, and then he'd moved just right, moved low and inside, instead of backing up like a damn amateur and taking the slug in the middle of the face. The guards had given Bennicke a start when they'd steamed down the road. For a minute he had thought they had come for him, and then he saw that they'd been going too fast to look at license plates, were interested only in hogging the ferry and getting across the river.

Stepping in to help the old doll when he'd seen her sick in the car had been a good gag. It had given him a chance

to get next to some strangers, get a good look at them. It
had given him the opening with the Mooney girl. And
that might shape up just right. The job was to get to San
Antone. Somehow it would work out. It had to work out.

He took a workmanlike satisfaction in the instinctive
way he had picked the right place to drop when he saw
the flicker of the revolver about to be used. The two flits
had raced down the river bank. The funny-looking little
guy had raced away from his twin blondes to hide behind
a tree. And that Mooney was all right. He'd seen her drift
quickly between two cars, moving the way people who
have seen trouble before learn how to move.

When Bennicke had heard and understood enough of
Texas' conversation with the fat politico to know the situation was over the hump, he had stood up and watched
with mild interest the way the eager guard was dis-
ciplined. There are a lot of ways to do a thing like that.
Bennicke admired their way. They split with the butts
and ripped with the sights, and that man was never going
to be entirely whole again. It was going to leave him just
a little unsure of himself. His manhood would leak out
through the ripped face and he would never again be the
sort of man you could trust, if he ever had been. It made
Bennicke remember the limey officer in Rangoon. One of
those apple-cheeked public-school boys. And if the liquor
deal was going to run right, they had to get his co-opera-
tion. Shike was running the show, and so he'd had the
limey kid beaten up three times on dark streets for no
reason at all, apparently, before they ever contacted him.
When they finally made the offer, the limey kid took it,
because the beatings had soured him just enough, had
given him a different slant on the wide world. A judicious
mauling at the right time could do a lot to promote a
future deal.

Bennicke saw the sick woman transferred to the second
sedan. The young couple got in with her and away they
went.

He sauntered down and talked with Texas for a little
while. It was easy to see what had made Texas jump. The
little silver-haired piece had given him just the right kind

of look. But Texas didn't seem to want to chat, and Bennicke gave him the needle a little about his gook blood, but it didn't take.

And then he saw the truck topple off the planks on the far side. It brought back all the fear. He knew he might be stuck in this damn place until daylight. And daylight would be murder—or punishment for murder. This afternoon the Mexico City papers had probably been loaded with it. God, what a play they'd give it! One of their little tight-pants bullfighters who wouldn't be wagging his cape in the Plaza México any more. The *aficionados* would want to see the murderer slowly flayed and broiled and basted with engine oil.

His hands were sweating. He ignored the way Mooney was looking at him and he turned away and climbed the bank and went as far away from other people as he could get and still stay in the shade, though with the slant of the sun, the shade wasn't as essential as it had been. The way that red ball was dropping, it was going to be night before you knew it.

Bennicke wondered if he was going to be sick. Just one break when you need it, and some featherhead drops his truck into the Río Conchos.

He crossed his legs and sat like a small muscular Buddha, flexing his fingers, trying to think of something quick and smart and bright. Something out of the bag of tricks. But the bag hung empty.

He watched sourly as Mooney came up the bank. The climb stretched the skirt of the yellow dress tightly, outlining her straight, thick, muscular thighs. Built for it, all right. All slut, and not to his taste, which ran to the restless, leaner, inbred wives of the roaming rich. He saw the pattern of them, of the two of them, as clearly as though he had already spent months with her. She would be the kind to slop around her apartment with tangled hair and crumby robe and busted slippers. Her cooking would come out of cans. And every now and again she would start whining and complaining and he would have to bounce her a little, the heel of the hand against the side of the face, to straighten her out. It made him feel tired to think of what the next few months would be like, even if he could get across the river.

She sat beside him with a heavy sigh. "Nice break, eh, Benson?"

"Thanks. I wouldn't have known if you hadn't told me."

"I've been thinking."

"Good for you."

"Take the chip off your shoulder," she said. She edged a bit closer and lowered her voice. "I've been thinking about your . . . troubles. You said you won't have a car and you'll have to get across the river the hard way. That little car isn't yours, huh?"

He gave her a long, hard look. "What are you dreaming up?"

"I've got the keys to the Buick. I'm supposed to take it across the river. But I can get somebody else to do it, I think."

"What have you got on your mind?"

She edged a little closer. "This guy I'm with. His name is Darby Garon. He's up there sleeping. See him?"

Bennicke looked up the hill, saw the man against a tree on the far side, chin on his chest. "So?"

"I don't know whether to say it because I don't know what you'll go for, Benson."

He saw, on her face, the excitement born of larceny. He knew he wasn't getting any ideas. Maybe she'd have a decent idea.

"I'm just a young fella trying to get along."

"If you get stuffy and tell him about it, I'll say you made it up."

"Keep talking."

"Look, I'm sick of the guy. And he's in a sling. He can't raise hell about anything. He's got a good job and a wife and kids in Houston. He wouldn't dare try to make trouble for me, no matter what I do. When the ferry comes back, all the cars will move down two places, right?"

"If it ever comes back."

"When you have to move your little car down, you can make out like it won't start. You can look under the hood and fool around, and then roll it over out of the way. The ditch is wide and shallow where you're parked. You can make it look good."

He nodded, narrowing his eyes. "I can do that," he said softly, testing the idea. It was obvious, and it wasn't bad.

"It will be dark then. I can get Darby off, away from the others. I can do that when it's nearly our turn to get across. And you follow us. Can you...knock him out without making any noise?"

"That isn't hard."

"He's got the car keys in his pocket, and his wallet is locked in the glove compartment. I think he's got about three or four hundred dollars left. I want all of that. You get his tourist card and the car papers. They're in the wallet. We tie him up or something, and go across on the ferry, and go right on across the bridge. We can drive right through to San Antone and put the car in a lot somewhere and go to my place."

"I don't look like him. I can't use his card."

"If you have to sneak out of the country, I think it's safer than trying any other way. My card will be O.K., and the car papers will be O.K. I can keep their eyes off you, sugar. And we can sprinkle a few pesos around. It will be late and they'll be tired. On the American side they'll go through the baggage, but they don't ask for any papers. You just have to make a declaration."

He stared down at his knuckles, thinking it over. It wasn't at all bad. And yet he didn't feel as if, in his state of exhaustion, he should trust his own judgment too much. It was good in one way. It would be a safer way of getting to Matamoros. The final decision could be made there, as to whether to risk crossing as Darby Garon. He remembered that they made you sign the tourist card when you surrendered it. He'd have a chance to scrawl Garon's signature a few practice times. It wouldn't have to be perfect.

"What can he do?" she asked softly.

"He can't do a damn thing about it."

"He won't even report the car stolen. He can't afford to."

"Let me think about it."

She moved closer again, so close that her breasts pressed against his upper arm. She increased the pressure slowly. "There any other arguments I can use, Del, honey?"

A twist of the wind brought the musky-ripe scent of her swirling full against his face. Desire superimposed itself on weariness, a knife with an oiled blade twisting slowly in his loins.

"Don't try to kid me," he said harshly. "Don't try to make me think you got other reasons. You want that four hundred bucks, and I'm just a way of getting it."

She moved away quickly. Anger flickered and faded. She grinned. "Is that bad?"

"What was wrong with my way?"

"This gets you across the river for sure. And we don't have to meet at that Rancho Grande, and I make sure he doesn't get funny and try to keep all that stuff he bought me."

"And I promised to be a ticket for the rent and the food and the liquor."

"O.K., we understand each other, Del."

"It might work."

"I took a chance, you know. Talking like this to you."

He gave her his jack-o'-lantern smile. "You take no chances. Not you. There's always a guy to hide behind."

"Once there wasn't. That's why I have to be careful."

"Do time for it?"

"Sixty days, but it could have been a one to five. I told Garon I worked in a phone office. That's a large laugh. Anyway, the time I got caught, I was working with a...friend. And he went out a window and they didn't get him, and there I was with more damn rolls of coins than you ever saw before. I bet there was eighty rolls of nickles. You should have seen me crying and yelling and saying I didn't know a darn thing about it."

Bennicke pursed his lips. "I don't like that. Those guys have a nasty habit of coming around and checking all the time, just for the laughs."

"Nuts. That was two years ago and it was over in El Paso. Besides, you said it was just Mexican trouble."

He made his shrug casual. "They might get real stuffy and try to get me extradited. But I doubt it."

"You could be bad news, Benson. I have a hunch."

"Then follow your hunch. Stop snowing in my face. Go and leave me alone."

She hit his knee gently with her fist. "It isn't much of a hunch."

He looked across the river. "There comes the answer to the Buick problem, anyway. Some guy is rowing her across."

Betty Mooney stood up. She smiled down at him. "Don't go away. I'll go give her the keys back."

Betty Mooney went down the bank. She gave Bennicke an oblique look, back over her shoulder. He saw that her knowledge of his eyes on her altered her walk a bit, put more of an arch in her back, made her slacken the thigh and hip muscles of the supporting leg with each step to increase the tilt and swing of the hefty hips. Watching her walk, he decided that the stay in San Antone might not be too expensive after all. She had slyness enough, but no real guts. There was a narrow line between amateur and pro. She could be broken down and put on the road. He'd made the same cool decision before, many times, and he had yet to be wrong. And once the yelping was over and they got used to it, their very abjectness made him feel bigger and stronger.

He knuckled his thigh. The damn tiredness was making him cross bridges before he came to them. The thing was to get out of this country. Maybe the brazen way was best. Brass it out. Take the Cad across the bridge. He fingered the reassuring bulge of the sweat-damp money belt. Money was your friend. Money and quickness and the bag of tricks.

He straightened out his tough bowed legs and leaned back, fingers laced against the harsh short hair at the back of his head. The sky was deepening. Once there was a color like that. When and where? A damn long time ago. Color of a shirt long ago in New Jersey, worn with a white tie. Hell, that's when I was pearl-diving in that stinking kitchen of that summer hotel. Just a kid. What was her

name, now? Dora? No, Dorine. Grabbed a swim early in
the morning off the hotel dock and there she was. Red
suit. Cute as a bug. A guest. She figured me as a guest too,
and I had sense enough not to talk too much. Dated her
for later, and bought that dark blue shirt in town. A real
sharp kid. What was I? Seventeen, I guess. About that.
Somehow they got wise. Her daddy and the manager were
waiting when I tried to sneak her back to the hotel.
Manager cracked me across the puss and fired me on the
spot. Nose bled on the white tie. Daddy dragged Dorine
inside and she was crying. Had to pack and get out right
then. That manager saw me off the grounds. Fooled them
all, though. Stashed the suitcase in the brush down the
road and sneaked back. Got gasoline out of the tool shed.
Poured it all over that big son-of-a-bitch of an automobile
her daddy had. A Pierce Arrow. Tossed the match and
ran like hell. God, what a whoompf!

Wonder what would have happened if they hadn't
caught us sneaking back. Never even tried to touch
Dorine. Thought she was an angel or something. Know
better now. Talk about turning points. Been roaming
ever since. Had to make time for a few days and get out
of the state. Wonder where Dorine is now. Home and
kids. Big eyes she had. Brown. Cute little mouth. Never
even touched her. Never even . . .

The hand on his shoulder brought him awake with a
start. The sky was black overhead, star-spangled.

"Sugar, your nerves are shot," Betty Mooney said,
laughter in her voice.

"Must have been asleep."

"Darby's still sleeping. And I don't wonder. That old
boy will sleep for a month to catch up."

He stared across the river. Spotlights had been rigged,
somehow. The truck was up on its wheels. Men were
hauling at a long rope and he heard the distant chant as
they heaved in unison. The truck was inching backward
out of the river.

"Progress, eh?"

"The ferry ought to be over pretty soon. And you'll
have to do something about your car."

He couldn't seem to come all the way up out of the mists of sleep. His mind was cottony, turgid. He stood up and stretched until he heard his shoulder muscles make small popping sounds.

"Who's singing?" he asked dully.

"Those twin blondes. Sitting up in their car. They gave me something. Here."

His hand closed around the cool bottle glass.

"It's tequila, sugar. Maybe you need some."

He removed the cork, tilted the bottle up. It splashed acidly against his teeth, burned his mouth. He took three gasping swallows, lowered the bottle, and shuddered. It socked hard into his stomach, made a spreading warmth.

He listened to the singing. Funny thing for them to be singing. Church music. Sounded sweet and clear. Gave you the creeps, somehow. Took you way, way back. Combed and brushed and sitting there, and the little shelves with holes for the wineglasses, and the funny taste of the bread as it melted slowly on your tongue. Sun slanting in and that low organ note that made your belly feel hollow every time the man hit that exact note.

Bad luck to think about churches.

He tilted the bottle up again. It went down easier.

"Hey, don't be a pig!"

He gave her back the bottle. Had to watch it. Empty stomach under that tequila. He braced his feet and stretched again, yawned, scrubbed at his belly with his knuckles.

She slid an arm under his and ran her fingers up the nape of his neck. He clamped her waist in his arm, put his mouth down hard on hers, pressing all substance out of it, pressing it into looseness, running his other hand down her flank, pulling her in hard against him.

"There's a place," she said, her voice sounding dusty and broken.

They stumbled back into the darkness, into the field behind the tree line, making difficult business of walking, the way he was holding her closely. After a time she turned against him, slack-legged, pulling him down, grass rasping dry under them, dress fabric rustling, then thighs hard-white in starlight, her mouth a blackness, eyes reflecting a feral star glint, and taloned hands and the fumbling and the knowledge of the quickness coming. Bennicke glanced to the side and saw, in the starlight, the bullfighter and the barb drawn back, and the metal gleam. With a great cry he threw himself back and away from her, scrabbling crabwise, crying out again, and suddenly the bullfighter was gone from the starlight. He looked at her and saw no barbed shaft protruding, saw only a whiteness and heard her voice, heavy with contempt, saying, "What the hell is the matter with you?"

He didn't answer. He located the gleaming bottle, set carefully aside out of harm's way. He moved to it, tilted it up, drained what was left.

"What am I supposed to do?" she asked acidly.

"Shut up!"

She sat up, rearranged her clothes. He threw the empty bottle into the darkness. It thudded and rolled, not breaking. When you started seeing things, you were going nuts. No question about that.

She moved to him, tried with a certain sullenness to excite him. He pushed her roughly away.

"The deal is off, sugar," she said.

"Just get away from me."

"Pardon me for living," she said. She got up and walked away, leaving him. He could still hear the sweet distant singing, the counterpoint chant from the far bank of the river. Something scuttled in the dry grass and he thought of scorpions and stood up, quickly. Desire had gone as though it had never existed, as though it would never return. The thought of her, the thought of any woman, sickened him.

Tequila rolled thunderously through his blood. He arched his hard thigh muscles and hunched his shoulders. He wanted to hit something, smash something, regain through violence his accustomed feeling of assurance.

After a bit he went down to the river bank, his walk a cocky strut, his elbows held away from his sides. Tequila droned and sang in his ears. The river bank was lighter because of the lights across the river. He saw the half-spick

Texan sitting with the pale-headed girl. The Texan's greaser buddy squatted on his heels a half-dozen feet from the couple, perennial cigarette clenched between thumb and middle finger. Flames roared high in Bennicke's brain. He had to do something, anything, to feel alive once more.

He swung his shoe and kicked the Texan's buddy heavily in the ribs, sending him sprawling. Bennicke bounced on his toes, waiting, and said, "Squat around where you don't get in people's way."

The Mexican jumped up and moved away, holding his hurt side. He said something softly to Texas, who had got to his feet.

Texas said gently, "What was the point in that?"

"He gets in my way and next time I kick him in the face."

Figures had moved out of the shadows. Bennicke felt them moving slowly in, converging on him. His mouth suddenly went dry. He suddenly realized he had to make his scrap with Texas, or perhaps feel the white-hot twist of a knife.

He moved with a prancing walk toward Texas, saying, "Maybe you want to get in my way?"

Texas said something quickly in Spanish. Laughter suddenly exploded through the tension, shattering it. The laughter went on and on. Bennicke felt his face burning.

"What kind of a crack was that?" he demanded. "You talk too fast for me."

"I told them they could watch how little fighting roosters are trained for the ring. Mrs. Gerrold, suppose you walk up the road and keep your back turned."

"I'll stay here, Bill," she said.

Bennicke realized that Danton expected to take him. So he leaped quickly, snatching at Danton's wrists, butting at his face. Danton snapped a hand free, brought his forearm across, chopping Bennicke across the side of the neck with it, moving his body out of the way. Del Bennicke's rush carried him to the side of the truck and he slammed his palms against it to stop himself.

He spun fast, bringing his hands up, but Texas hadn't followed him. He stood, waiting for Bennicke to make the next move, and Bennicke sensed contempt and anger in the tall man. Bennicke put his chin on his chest and went in fast, trying to hook the taller man in the middle. From somewhere out of the night there came a vast, hard-knuckled fist, swung like a bag of rocks on the end of a rope. He saw it a fraction of a second too late—too late to roll with it, much too late to move inside of it. As red lights exploded across the sky, and as the earth tilted up to crash against the back of his head and shoulders, he was filled with anger at his own mistake in judgment, yet also with the release that only violence seemed able to bring him.

When he sat up, Texas was sitting on his heels talking to the girl again. Texas said, "Now tell my friend you're sorry. The one you kicked."

"You can scrap," Bennicke said softly.

"Tell him."

Bennicke found Pepe in the gloom. "Sorry," he grumbled.

"*Está bien,*" Pepe said, and Bennicke heard the laughter behind his words. Bennicke got up slowly, kneading the side of his neck. They all seemed to be waiting for his reaction, looking at him as if he was a damn beetle in a jar. He walked away, up the dark road.

The Mooney girl caught his arm, pulled him away from a nearby car. She was panting as though she had run a long way. Almost like a dog in summer.

"What the hell's wrong with you?"

"Del, oh, my God, Del!" she whispered, holding his arms. "He's . . . he's dead! And I thought he was asleep!"

He pushed her away. "It's your party. Remember? I'm out of it."

"You're not! You're not! You're going to help me."

"In a pig's—"

"Because if you don't, I'll tell everybody here the Mexican cops want you. I'll get somebody to tell them in Matamoros. I'll tell them you stole that car. I'll tell them you're a murderer or something. I'll clobber you good if you don't help me."

"O.K.," he said quickly. He took her up the steep bank, and in the deeper blackness near the trees, he drove his right hand at her throat, caught the softness between thumb and strong fingers. She raked his face once before he pinned her hands. She twisted and they tripped and went down, heavily. She thrashed, half under his weight, and then he sensed her struggling growing weaker. Suddenly he released the pressure, sat a bit apart from her, his head in his arms. She coughed and gagged for a time, then lay still, breathing hard.

In a husky, toneless voice she said, "What made you quit?"

"I don't know."

"They must want you bad, the Mexican cops."

"They do."

"Murder?" she whispered.

"It wasn't, but they'll call it that."

"We're both in bad shape, Del."

It was said in a quiet voice, a voice that held no anger, no surprise.

"How do you know he's dead?"

She took his hand and he felt her shiver. "I went to him. He was making a real funny noise. I couldn't figure it. And then . . . something ran away from him. Something small. It was . . ."

He had a funny impulse to put his arm around her. Comfort her, somehow. All the brass and starch was gone out of her. She was a frightened kid.

"I'll help," he said, "but not on account of you threatening me. Keep that straight."

"I don't care why as long as you do it."

"We'll do it just like we planned. Only I'll have to get him away from here. I'll have to carry him. I remember from daylight that there's a rock ridge about a quarter mile back and a half mile off the road—same side of the road he's sitting on. I can get him up on my shoulders. We'll drag him back a way so nobody will notice. I'll put him over behind that ridge. It should work. They'll find his car in San Antone. The records will show he came back into the States. I'll strip him, and if nobody finds him before tomorrow night, they'll never know who the hell he was—or even what color he was."

On the far side of the river the truck was completely out of the way. Two cars had crawled up to the ferry deck. Bennicke sat silently, thinking of how close he had come to killing her, of killing, with her, his only chance. Murder had been the word to touch off the insanity. They were all after him. Every one of them. Even now somebody was probably watching. He looked around, moving his head very slowly.

Chapter Eleven

WHEN he had seen Linda's bright hair in the lowering sunlight, bright against the muddy river, Bill Danton, the tall Texan, had felt a stir of pleasure so quick and so warm that it startled him a bit. It matched the pang of regret he had felt watching the ferry pull away, taking her out of his life for keeps.

He remembered Dad saying that the surest way to get to like people was to do them a favor. They might resent you, but you sure got fond of them quick. He wondered if the Quixote job had been what warmed him up toward her. She was a cute little bug, all right, with that hair lighter than her golden shoulders, and that look of hers, grave like a little kid, but yet showing that she was a woman grown. The tan linen dress hung sweetly on her, deftly accenting the taut little hips, commenting briefly on the cone-sharpness of her young breasts. He had sensed that here was that rare and lovely thing, a woman with beauty but also with loyalty, sensitivity, and the funny humor which is at once lusty and pixie. Her laughter would be wry bells, and there would always be a part of her that could never be completely captured, thus taking from any relationship with her that dull curse of possessiveness.

He guessed he had better face up to it and admit, watching the shabby rowboat approach the bank, that she was just too darn close to that picture he had been carting around in his head, of a girl he had never met, of a girl made up of bits and pieces of other girls known wisely and not too well.

He walked down to the bank, pulled the bow of the rowboat up, gave her his hand. She came out of the boat onto the gray cracked bank and told him very calmly that her mother-in-law had died. And suddenly her mouth twisted and her face contorted like the face of a child. He put his arm around her shoulders, walked her away from the line of cars, walked her upstream along the river bank. She took tissue from her purse, and when he began to sense a warning rigidity of her shoulders, he took his arm away quickly. She sniffled at intervals and finally stopped and planted her feet and blew her nose.

"Darn foolishness," she said in a small voice, smiling weakly.

"Not at all. It can be a hell of a shock."

"It was, but I don't think I was crying for her. I never really got to know her. We've only been married a few weeks, and she tried to stop us from being married, until she saw she couldn't win, and then she got very sweet about it. She flew down to Mexico City to travel back with us to Rochester. It was a shock because . . . well, she was such a strong personality. In her own quiet way."

They came to a tree that had been brought down in some flood of long ago. The trunk was bleached white by the sun. She sat down on the trunk, her chin resting on her palm, elbow on her knee.

Bill thought of the young husband. Just a kid. This girl had grown up, but he hadn't quite managed it yet. He sat down on the trunk, handed over a cigarette.

"I've got some here, thanks," she said.

"Talking can help, you know. I listen good."

"I don't want to cry on your shoulder, Mr. Danton."

"Bill. And I heard your husband call you Linda. Is it O.K. if I do?"

"Certainly, Bill. This is a crazy day. As if the world had stopped. I feel as though I were dreaming it. The doctor gave me something to take and the world is all fuzzy. If I start talking, I won't stop. I can feel it. And I'll say too much and get a load of remorse later."

"That truth serum they use, isn't that just a sedative? Sodium something. Sodium pentothal."

"How is anybody supposed to know what truth is?"

"Well, I haven't talked metaphysics since a couple of required courses at A. and M., but maybe I can remember just a little. As I remember it, some people claim that truth, as such, is not a constant. It varies with the individual and with the time and the place. Say like what was true yesterday is a damn lie tomorrow."

"Maybe I've hit a place in my life where I've got to change my ideas about truth. That ever happen to you?"

"Sure has, Linda. Had to change everything once when I was a kid. My stepmother is a Mexican lady. When I first went to the States to school, I had the damnedest accent you ever heard. Anybody called me a Mexican, I had to go down fighting. Did a lot of fighting, all right. One day I wondered what in the pure hell I was fighting about. Next boy that called me a Mexican, I told him I was. Made me feel better. Made me feel better than fighting, because when I was fighting it was like I was objecting to the label. World is full of people objecting to labels. Washington is full of people calling each other communists."

"Your home is happy, isn't it, Bill? Are you married?"

"No, I live with the folks. What makes you think it's happy?"

"Oh, it's an air people have. I don't know. Sort of secure. When I was little we had a happy home. Dad died and it sort of broke up, and I guess ever since I've been trying to get married so I could re-create life the way it was. My husband's home life wasn't happy. I think I wanted to give him what I had, and what he missed."

"We get along fine. Big stone hacienda sort of place near Mante. Always somebody singing. Always a laugh. We give each other a bad time, but let somebody else try to, and the Dantons unite."

"That's the way it should be."

He frowned. "Maybe it's just *too* good. I've been doing a lot of thinking today. I get restless, but I never get the gumption to pull out and do anything on my own."

She looked down at the gray hard mud near her feet. He looked at her and saw the tears begin to spill out of her eyes again. "Hey, now!" he said softly.

"I...I can't seem to help it. We're alone. I won't ever see you again. If I can blow off steam, maybe I...can stop getting the weeps every minute."

"I told you before. I listen good."

"But this is so personal, damnit." She took more tissue and wiped her eyes. "How is a person to know anything? I fell in love with my husband. As far as I knew, I was in love for keeps, and it couldn't hit harder. Oh, a dream world! With violins and roses, yet. And today I find out that inside he's really sort of a—a little person. I'm trying to talk myself back in love with him, but I can't seem to."

"He's probably upset. Hell, he's just a kid."

She gave him a look of surprising fury. "I like kids. I want to have a lot of my own and raise them. I don't want to bring up somebody else's."

"Maybe this thing today will make him grow up."

"I doubt it. And see where it leaves me, Bill? What do I do now? Go ahead and try to make the best of it, and maybe leave him five years from now after he's taken all the joy out of life? Or quit right now? I have a lot of respect for marriage. I wanted mine to last forever. You start treating marriage like a . . . like a car you can trade in when you get tired of it, and it doesn't have much meaning any more. And I can't blame John Carter Gerrold for what he is. It's his mother's fault. Do you want to hear a good definition of a bore? It's one of Dad's."

"Sure."

She spread her arms wide, like a fisherman recalling the one that got away. She was holding up her two index fingers. She waggled the one on the left hand. "Now, here is what you think you are, see?" She waggled the index finger of the right hand. "And here is what you actually are. If the two things are way apart like this, you get a bore, somebody who can't see himself as others see him. The closer together you bring the two hands, the better sort of person you represent. If you actually are what you think you are, with the fingers right together like this, then the chances are that you're a pretty decent human being. A nice guy. Dad used to say that most of us have just a little divergence, and that if a man didn't have any, maybe he wouldn't have any pride."

"Sounds like your father was a pretty shrewd guy."

"He was. I keep thinking, though, that I can do the same thing to explain to myself what's happened. Over here is what I thought John was. And over here is what he actually is. I had fun fooling myself, all right, but now in one day I've found out what he actually is and I don't like it. I don't want to live with it. Then I wonder if I'm being a perfectionist or something."

"It's hard for me to say, looking at it from the outside."

"I know why he married me. In my own way, I guess I'm just as tough underneath as his mother was. And he needs to have someone strong. He's got so he depends on strong people. He thinks he's just a little more acute and sensitive and perceptive than anybody else in the world."

"Can he make a living?"

"As a sort of pensioner. His uncle will give him a job. A good job. He won't ever have to worry. I could still go along with the plan. Go back to Rochester with him and buy or build a little house in a very nice section and belong to the Genesee Valley Club and the Rochester Country Club and play a brisk game of backgammon and be that charming young hostess, Mrs. John Carter Gerrold the Second. And now I wonder if in about six months I wouldn't be ready to spit. It would be fine if I could just . . . get back in love with him."

"But you don't think you can, eh?"

She lit another cigarette. The last of the sun was gone. The lighter flame seemed surprisingly bright against the blue-purple dusk.

"Bill, I've always had sort of an instinct about people. And I've never been so wrong as with my husband. Right now I wouldn't want him to—to touch me. It would make me feel creepy. I'm talking too much."

"Like you said, you won't see me again."

She glanced toward him quickly. "No, I won't."

Her words were flat and they seemed to open a small trap door in the bottom of his soul. A world where he wouldn't see her again, ever, suddenly seemed to be a sour place. He told himself he was going too fast. You didn't fall in love in an afternoon. Or fall out of love. That was for the movies.

And he suddenly thought of a way he could say it to her, a way that wouldn't be rude. He spoke at once. "Now look, you're wondering if you can really fall out of love with your husband, just like that." He snapped his fingers.

"I guess that's the question."

"Well, let's get hypothetical, then. Could this happen? That I could see you and talk to you a little bit and then see you coming back across the river and get a feeling in my stomach just like Christmas Eve when I was a kid? Could it be possible for me to think of no place on earth I want to be more than just here sitting and talking to you? Is it possible that right now, the way you sit there, your hair so light in the darkness makes my heart keep turning right over, and keeps drying my mouth up? And makes me feel that you're wasted on a kid like that, and I want you for myself?"

She stood up quickly, facing him, her hands tight on her purse. "No, Bill. That couldn't happen."

He stood up too, stood a step from her, looking down into her eyes. "It can be the truest thing you ever heard of," he said.

"I didn't want you to say that."

"I didn't know I was going to say it until you said that you'd never see me again, and I knew I had to say it quick. You think you're all mixed up. How about me?"

"Bill, this is . . ."

He put his hands on her shoulders, leaned slowly toward her lips. She offered them, and there was just enough light for him to see her eyes close as he kissed her. She broke the kiss by spinning away from him. With her back to him, she laughed. It was a very ugly laugh.

"I must be breaking some kind of record. I've had this dress off once today. I don't want you thinking I'm ready to take it off again. It wrinkles so easily."

He stared at her rigid back. "Honey, you're trying to hurt me, and you're just hurting yourself."

"I've got a new question. How cheap can a girl get?"

"Don't talk that way. It isn't right for you to say a thing like that."

"How do you know I don't always talk this way?"

"Because I know you, Linda. I know you well, as if I'd

been with you for years. Now tell me we won't ever see each other again."

"We won't, my friend. I promise you that."

He took a deep breath. "Maybe we ought to be wandering back to the others."

She turned, smiled. "Thanks, Bill."

They walked slowly back. Floodlights came on on the far side of the river. She said, "I've got to get the car keys back from the Mooney girl."

"No hurry about that. She isn't going anywhere."

He opened the door of the pickup, spread a blanket on the running board for her. He sat on his heels near her. It puzzled him a bit. He hadn't meant to say as much as he did. Once the words started coming, it was as though he couldn't stop them. Not fair to give her another mess to deal with. Let her get one out of the way first. Pepe'd said that kid husband had slugged her one, up in the store. No matter how upset the kid was, there was no excuse for that. Her lips were still a bit swollen. Guess she was using psychology, with that crack about the dress. Trying to scare the guy off.

He remembered when they had walked downstream, a few hours ago. Had a blanket with them. Looked happy enough. Well, newlyweds were maybe expected to do that sort of thing. It made his neck feel hot to think of the two of them on that blanket. Kid husband didn't know what he had. Made him feel jealous, too. Crazy jealous. Wanted to bash somebody.

He said, "I should have kept it to myself."

"It doesn't matter. In a week you won't remember what I look like."

"I won't ever forget what you look like."

"Please."

"I just wanted to set you straight on that, Linda."

"I've probably got the instincts of a tramp. So skip it."

"You need thinking time. That's what you need. There's a hotel in Matamoros that isn't too bad. You could hole up there and Pepe and I could make a fast trip to Houston. Your tourist card doesn't run out for quite a while, does it?"

"No, but—"

"And then Pepe and I, we could run you down to Mante. Easy day's drive from Matamoros and the pickup doesn't run too bad. The folks would be glad to have you, and there's plenty of room."

"No, I—"

"Let me finish. I promise not to get in your hair. I won't pop off like I did back there on that log. If you get a hankering to go on back to him, why, then you can go right ahead, with no harm done."

"Bill, that's sweet of you, but I should at least stay with John until . . . everything is taken care of. That's only decent."

"Guess you're right about that. But you could come back, couldn't you?"

"I don't want to talk about it."

Pepe was sitting on his heels, politely out of earshot. Bill saw the man named Benson come down the road. He knew from the sway of the cocky walk that the man was drunk. But he was not prepared for the brutal kick, for Pepe's gasp of pain, for the man's crazy belligerence. He saw the other Mexicans drifting toward Benson and knew that the long boredom of the day had bred violence, knew that not long before there had been blood, and a brutal beating. Benson acted a little crazy.

So he made the joke about the fighting rooster and all the others laughed, because Benson's attitude was comically like that of one of the strutting birds.

Bill had fought at college, and later in the Navy. He knew that a good bigger man could readily take care of a good smaller man. And the brutality of the kick, the philosophy behind it, sickened him. Linda, to his surprise, preferred to stay.

The butting almost caught him off guard. He gave Benson a chance to turn and come back in. He noted, even as he sucked his stomach away from a whistling hook and used the left to set the man up, that Benson knew what he was doing. He had no wish to break his hand, so he hit hard at the solid neck just under the ear. Benson tumbled like a doll thrown by a careless child. Bill

Danton sucked his knuckles for a moment, watching to see if Benson would get up, then went over and sat on his heels where he had been before.

"Why did you want to stay around?" he asked.

"I was going to take off my shoe and hit him with it if he got you down. I never saw anything so dirty mean in my life, the way he kicked Pepe."

"Pepe's just another Mexican," Bill said softly.

She cocked her head on one side. "Don't try any of your tests on me, my friend. I'm one-eighth Cherokee. We Indians are a persecuted minority."

"You know, that's the first time I've really heard you laugh, Linda. Knew just how it was going to sound, too."

"Not again, Bill!"

"Walk up the road with me. I want to talk just a little bit more. It won't hurt you to listen."

"The ferry looks about ready to start back."

"Pepe will put the truck on. You're meeting your husband in San Fernando?"

"No, he's gone on with . . . the body. Maybe by now he's got across the river with her."

"You aren't planning to take that Buick all the way to Matamoros?"

"I'm a big girl now."

He spoke to Pepe. Pepe grinned slyly, bobbed his head.

"What did you say to him?"

"I told him which cantina to stay in in Matamoros and that I was driving you there."

"Now, really, Bill, I'm perfectly capable of—"

"There are plenty of places in the States where I wouldn't want to see a pretty girl have car trouble and have to stop and try to flag another car."

"I'll be *perfectly* all right!"

"Even driving up those planks? Pretty narrow."

"Well . . . maybe that might be . . ."

"It's all settled. Come on. Let's see who's singing. Sounds nice."

The blonde twins were in the last car in line. Between songs one of them said, "Come on. Anybody can get in. This time another oldie. 'Moonlight Bay.'"

They leaned against the car. Linda sang a clear alto part. The lights strung outside the store touched her face. Bill sang along with the three girls. In the shadow of the car he found Linda's hand. Without interrupting her singing, she tried to pull it away. He held it tightly. And then he saw her smile as she sang, saw her shoulders lift in a tiny shrug. She left her hand in his, curled small. Bill sang in a rusty baritone that he tried to keep as inaudible as possible. There was a magic in the night, and in the old song, and in their voices. Some other tourists joined in, not coming closer, singing at a distance. Magic in having her close to him. Near the end of the song she moved unconsciously closer to him, her shoulder touching his arm. The song ebbed and they all laughed for no reason, and Linda choked off her laughter quickly. He knew that she was remembering the death, and thinking how callous it was to forget so easily.

Headlights went on at the front of the line and they heard motors starting up. The ferry came in and there was no need to shovel at the river bottom to work it close enough. But the planks still had to be used. It took much shouting and advice to get them spaced and blocked to everybody's satisfaction.

Two cars came off the ferry and went up the road, horns bleating, people shouting from the cars and at the cars. They watched the MG drive aboard, and then the pickup truck. The planks and blocks were heaved aboard and the ferry moved slowly off across the river.

"It ought to move faster now," Bill said.

"Release my hand, sir. Ain't fittin' for a married lady."

"Sorry."

"Much obliged."

They walked down the road. Cars were moving down to take up the spaces vacated. The whole line moved. Bill saw that Benson was having trouble with his car. He couldn't seem to get it started.

He stopped and said, "Anything I can do?"

Benson was astonishingly cordial. "Hell, no. Should have had the fuel pump replaced before I tried the trip. Help me ease her out of the way and I'll lock her up.

Leave her here and come back *mañana* with the replacement, if I can find one."

The car rolled easily on the grade. Benson tucked it in close to the bank, started rolling up the windows. "I guess I was a little crocked when I kicked your pal."

"You want to watch that. It's a good way to start looking like a pincushion."

"Yeah. Fool stunt."

"Need a ride?"

"No, I'm all fixed up. That you, Mrs. Gerrold? Didn't see you in the dark. How's your mother-in-law making it?"

"She died, Mr. Benson, just when we got her to the doctor."

"That Mooney girl thought she would. Sorry to hear it. Say, here's the keys to the Buick. I was going to move it down for you. Still will, if you want me to. Guess you want the keys back, don't you?"

"Please."

He got out of the car, handed them to her, turned, and locked the doors of the Humber.

Bill and Linda walked to the Buick. Bill moved it down two spaces. Linda said, "Who's been talking to friend Benson? Dale Carnegie?"

"It's a little fishy, I think."

"What do you mean?"

"I know the type. They get sweet as pie just before they pull something raw."

"Then be careful of him, dear. What am I *saying*? Dear, indeed."

"You don't know how good it sounded."

"I wonder who he's riding with, Bill."

"With the Mooney girl, I'll give odds. And the Mooney girl's overage boy friend. You know, he seemed very relieved that you'd take the keys back. Almost too happy about it. And I never saw anybody get taken sober so fast. Want to sing some more?"

"Let's!" Then she sighed. "But I really shouldn't."

"I don't think it matters too much."

"But no hand-holding, huh?"

"If you insist."

They walked toward the music, through the night magic. I, William, take thee, Linda. Rough, maybe, to be a second husband. Second in line. Maybe, after a bad marriage, you did better. He knew they would have met, sooner or later, somehow. And just a few weeks too late. Bless her. Take time, but sooner or later she would know, and it would hit her as hard as it had hit him.

Chapter Twelve

Betty Mooney stood in the shallow ditch below the bank, a big frightened girl in a wilted yellow dress. She was horribly conscious of the body ten feet behind her, rigid in the tree shadows. God, what a desperate, miserable mess!

Del Benson had gone to get his car out of the way, leaving her with...it. Gee, he had seemed like such a cute, cute little guy with those big shoulders and the toughie face and that black bristly hair she wanted to feel of. A nice way to unhook from that stupe, Darby Garon. Darby Garon was gone. And the thing up on the bank had a new, evil sort of life for her.

Never liked bodies. Some people seem to be able to take them or leave them. Like undertakers.

An old memory came back and she shivered. That was the summer I was fifteen. Just turned fifteen. Anybody'd take me for eighteen. Well, that Graham girl, right down the road, we kept talking that spring about doing it, and what it would be like, and her big sister had told her how to stay out of trouble, and we would talk until we like to bust about how it would be, doing it with all the different boys we knew, talking about each one and maybe what he'd say, until that spring we giggled ourselves damn near silly, but getting that hot feeling, all sweaty, just thinking about it.

And we kept going over to the old Murphy place near the creek, where the house burned down and they moved away, and there was dry stale hay in the loft, and one day Sally Graham and I, we undressed and we were talking about it and we sort of fooled with each other until we got shy and creepy and funny-acting, and that was, I suppose, why I told Gubby Garfield, that hot day he asked me to go swimming, that there was a good hole in the creek near the old Murphy place, and he said he'd never

133

heard of any hole over there, that it wasn't much above
your knees because he'd fished it all and he knew, if anybody knew.

But I told him there certainly was a hole because I'd
swum in it, and deep enough for diving, probably. That
old car of his had no fenders and boxes to sit on instead
of a seat, I remember, and no sides or top, and he called it
the strip-tease job. In the little side pocket of the bag
where I had the suit and the towel, I had two of the
things Sally had stole off her sister, and I was scared and
jumpy all the way out there. We changed to our suits off
in the bushes, and I couldn't joke around like always,
and then I had to pretend I couldn't find the swimming
hole, while he got sort of mad. And we swam anyway,
finally, with our fingers scraping the bottom all the time,
and sometimes bumping a knee. It was a real hot day.

Just testing him out, sort of, I said we ought to be
swimming without suits on a day so hot, and he gave me
a look like he was going to hop in his car and run for
cover, so I knew it had to happen a different way. Fifteen
he was, too, and I remember that because of our birthdays
being so close together.

We swam up the creek a way, like exploring, and he got
over being mad that there was no hole to dive in, because
he was a good diver. And then that storm came over the
hill like a freight train, soaking our clothes before we
could get back to them, and it was like it was all planned.
Weather changed fast, and I said we ought to go in the
Murphy barn and get our clothes dried out. We ran for
it, and our teeth were chattering, and he kept yaking
about his motor getting all wet. And we went up in the
loft on the stale hay and hung the clothes on nails to dry,
and he started kissing me, and then he got all jumpy too,
and we took off our suits and did it, and he hadn't ever
done it before, but he knew how the little things worked.
It didn't hurt a bit, but it didn't feel very good either,
like I thought it was going to. We talked about doing it,
and then we talked about swimming and diving, and
then about his car, and then he got so he wanted to do it
again and I said no and he said what difference did it

make if it happened once anyhow, so I couldn't see any good argument to tell him, so I let him start doing it again, and I was thinking how silly a damn-fool thing it was to do, and how dopey we'd look there to anybody watching, and then it started to be different than the first time and that fool barn like to tipped up and thrown me right up into the sky. It broke me all in little pieces and stirred up the pieces with a spoon. I came back to earth and he was griping about the way I'd stuck fingernails in him and chewed his shoulder and like to killed him. I knew I certainly couldn't wait to get back to Sally Graham and tell her we were all wrong about it, because there weren't any words for how it was, because nobody has ever made up the right words.

The clothes were almost dry and we came down out of the loft, and instead of going out the door we'd come in, he wanted to get a look at his car, and we went out the small door, past where there were beat-up box stalls, and there was Sally Graham in the blue dress I liked so much, turning slow because a little wind was coming in, and one of her shoes had fallen off near the keg she'd kicked over, her face turned sideways and a funny blue kind of black, and her tongue stuffed out of her mouth, swollen like the toe on a rubber boot.

I guess I just dropped my bag with my swimming suit in it and I ran with the screaming hysterics and I must have gone a mile before I fell down and skinned my knee good. Gubby Garfield came along in the car and I got in and we went to town and told Myron Hattley, the chief of police. I couldn't stop thinking of her hanging and swinging down there while we were right up over her head, doing it. And I'd never get a chance to tell her, and anyway, it wasn't Sally any more, just like that thing up on the bank behind me isn't Garon any more.

Finally I found out from her big sister that the little tart had been getting it from the Granton's hired man, and when she'd gone down to the city it was to see a doc who told her she was pregnant. They damn near lynched the hired man, but he got out in time.

Maybe if all that hadn't happened, maybe I'd have got

married the next year or so, and settled down like my
sisters did. But seeing her swinging there, it made it seem
like life is too short a thing to get yourself tied up with
some jerk who wants you for the sleeping and the cooking. Anyway, a couple of weeks later, Gubby and I, we
started doing it again, but I wouldn't go back to the Murphy place and he found a shed near where a man was
building a big place and ran out of money, and Gubby
busted the lock on the shed and fixed it so that it still
looked locked. We kept taking stuff in there after dark,
and after a while it was fixed up nice. We were even figuring how we could heat the place when it got cold, and I
guess probably we overdid it, because Gubby kept saying
how his mother kept cramming food down him and complaining about how thin and jumpy he was getting, and
finally they sent him to a doctor, and the doctor must
have worried the hell out of Gubby somehow, because
Gubby told him what we'd been doing and the doc talked
to Ma and she laid it on my tail so good she took out
pieces of hide. But we sneaked away again and got caught
and Gubby's family sent him to live with his aunt in the
city, and word really got around that time. Ma just acted
discouraged and I didn't get laced after we got caught
that way.

The damn town was dull and I got out the next year,
and got that crumby waitress job in El Paso, telling them
I was twenty.

Well, the world is full of cheap guys who think perfume from J. C. Penney is a big deal, and lately I've been
wondering why I just don't go ahead and peddle it, but
that makes you a whore. And then after all the cheapies,
along comes this Darby Garon, and I've never seen anybody's tongue hanging out so far. This was the best one
of all, with the twelve hundred bucks' worth of stuff
I've got in that Cad. That Darby was a funny guy. Half
the time I had to pretend I understood what he was talking about. He was a real beaver, and then all of a sudden
he goes flat. Damn it, if this gets out, even if I didn't have
anything to do with it, it means cops, and cops mean
checking back on that old record, and it means trouble,

and with a character that important, I'll get a year and a day just for laughs. One year of starch and laundry work will turn me into a glamour-puss for sure.

It's got to be that Benson. He's got to get me out of it. And his trouble is bad. It's got him a little nuts. He jumped off like I was about to burn him. And I wanted it, too. More than any time I can remember. He's such a cute muscley little character. He knows I can fix him good. He damn near fixed me, too. My throat still hurts.

Why doesn't he come back? If I have to stand here thinking of that thing behind me, I'm going to start screaming. He's got to get me out of this. We'll have to take a chance at the bridge. I won't drive that Cad across. Not in a million years. I'll walk and I'll leave the twelve hundred bucks' worth of clothes and things.

She jumped violently as he came up beside her. "Give me some warning, will you?"

"Shut up. I gave the keys back to the girl. That ferry is working good now. I rolled the Cad down to where it belongs. We got to do it between ferry trips."

"Del, I'm scared. I'm scared green."

"Stay right where you are. I'm going to drag him back a ways, and if anybody moves too close, cough loud. When I'm ready for you, I'll whistle. Good thing they're singing. Covers up the noise."

He moved away up the bank, walking quietly. She stood with her elbows in her palms, shoulders hunched. Dear God, I didn't mean anything like this to happen. Maybe I've been a tramp, but I haven't really hurt anybody. They all want it, and it doesn't do any harm, and this one wanted it more than anybody else. And he didn't care if I went out and bought the clothes. It didn't make any difference to him. He'd stopped thinking about money or about anything else except doing it, like he'd gone a little crazy or something, and then he started to think of the money, and in his sleep he kept saying Moira, Moira. That must be his wife. And those kind are the worst, maybe, the ones who never take a little cheat, and then get it all wound up inside them, the kind that take money out of banks and run away. I didn't mean to hurt anybody, even that Moira I've never met, and if I can just get out of this, just get clear of it, maybe things will be different. Maybe way back I was wrong, and what I should have is kids and one guy, and it could still be that way because I've never been sick and I could have kids.

But it could be a dirty trick on the guy because you get used to thinking about different ones, and I could go right back to the same old thing.

Sally died and Darby died, and there was the time I saw that wreck. Riding back from Dallas with the big Polack. I can't remember his name, but on his arm he had a woman tattooed with a snake going around and around her and he could make the muscle in his arm move so that she moved so you had to laugh. And that car full of kids went by us doing maybe ninety, and I could see it clear, the way when they cut in the wheels on one side lifted real slow and they seemed to keep going on forever with those wheels up in the air and then the wheels came down quick and hard and the car went quick across the road and hit that bank and went up in the air as high as a roof and we had the brakes on but we went by and I could look across and see that one girl, hanging in the sky with her arms and legs kicking like in the comedy cartoons where the little animals run back onto the cliffs when they find out they're in mid-air.

I kept yelling to the big Polack to keep on going and I didn't want to see it. But no, he had to back up and pile out of the car and I wasn't going to look, but I had to. Funny how you have to look right at something awful when you don't want to. I went over and the car was like you'd taken it in your fist. Five of them and three already dead and the big Polack grunting and trying to stop the girl from bleeding but there wasn't enough left of her arm to tie anything on it and she died too. And like a miracle that one boy walking around with his clothes torn. Just walking and looked way off toward the horizon like he was expecting something, like waiting at an airport. The trucks stopped and when I saw the truck driver being sick, I was sick too, and when the Rangers came we said we came along after it happened, because you see a thing like that happen and tell them and you have to appear in court. When they tried to put the boy in the ambulance, they had to sit on him and tie him up. It took three big men and he wasn't a big boy.

Funny how I never liked the Polack after that, and pretty soon he got sick of asking, and I never went up to Dallas with him again.

Seeing dead ones makes you think of being dead and how you will look and what people will say about you. I don't ever want to die. I want to keep living until they find something you can take so you won't die.

She heard the soft whistle. She turned obediently and went up the bank. She couldn't see Benson. He whistled again and she followed the sound. He'd dragged the body back about fifty feet from the tree. The starlight seemed brighter back beyond the roadside line of trees. Darby Garon was on his side, his knees pulled up.

"Once I get him on my shoulders I can carry him. You got to help me get him up there."

"I won't touch him."

"You got to or I won't help you. I'll tell you what to do."

He lifted the body into a semi-upright position, stooped and dug his shoulder into the stomach, and said, "Now, I want him to fall forward across my shoulders. Don't let him slip off."

She tried to help. She pushed her palms straight out in front of her. She recoiled from the touch and the body slipped and fell. Benson cursed her.

He tried again. This time she managed to support the body as he grunted up to his feet. The body lay face down across his shoulders. Benson had one arm locked around a leg, the two wrists held in the other hand.

There was strain in his voice as he said, "Now walk slow in front of me and let me know if anything's in the way."

She could hear the singing. "The Devil and the Deep Blue Sea." Benson stumbled and cursed. He said. "Keep off to the right. Aim for that ridge of rocks over there."

The very faint light in the western sky outlined the ridge. She rubbed the palms of her hands down her thighs. She had touched a body with those hands.

Benson walked heavily, not speaking. Once he grunted, "Off to the right more so we come around behind it."

"There's a big stone here, Del."

They circled the ridge. Her eyes were used to the night and she saw a sheltered sandy place. "Is this all right?" she asked, turning to look at him. He lifted his head a bit and looked around. He turned around and took a couple of cautious backward steps, then straightened, releasing the body. It fell from his shoulders onto the sand, landing flat on its back. Benson ground at the small of his back with his fists. He knelt, pulled off the shoes and socks, pulled off the shorts, ripped the shirt off. He emptied the pockets of the shorts into his own. She heard the jangle of the car keys. She wanted to turn away from the body. It lay pale in the starlight, with blackness around the belly.

Benson balled up the clothes and set them aside. He knelt beside the body and the sudden flare of the lighter flame startled her. Black turned to brown-red.

"A bullet in the gut!" Benson said, wonderingly. He snapped out the light. Her night vision was gone. She stood in an impenetrable blackness.

"Honey pie, you wouldn't have shot your old daddy, would you?"

"No!" she cried. "No!"

"Wait a minute! The angle would be right. What do you know! That shot that Texas ducked. Went right up the slope of the road and into this guy. I don't get it. Hell, he could have rolled down the bank or something or yelled to get attention. It didn't kill him when it hit him. So he just sat there and died."

"Del! Then we can say how it happened! We can tell people!"

"Don't be more of a damn fool than you can help. You think that big shot is going to step up and say one of his men fired the shot? You think you're going to get any backing from the people around here? You better treat it just as if you'd shot him, honey. Let's get away from him."

They walked back toward the glow of lights. He stopped by a big rock. He dropped the bundle of clothes. "Wait here a minute."

She waited. He wasn't gone long. "What did you do?" she asked.

"Wrist watch." He grabbed the edge of the big rock. She heard the crackle of muscles and the rock shifted. He dropped to his knees, and, digging the way a dog does, scooped out a hole. He jammed the clothes into the hole, covered it over, shifted the rock back, dusted his hands, gave a satisfied grunt.

With each thing he did she found she was becoming more dependent on him. He was using his head, making the decisions. They reached the top of the bank. Car motors were starting up again. The ferry, lanterns burning aboard, slid toward shore.

"They'll find him," she said. "They'll find him."

"Sure they will, honey. Something will find him tonight, and some other things will find him in the morning, and the ants will finish the job."

"Don't," she said faintly.

"You got to ride your luck, ride all the luck you can get. Here's what we do. We take the Cad to San Antone. Maybe somebody knows the two of you and saw you together. So we check you out of your apartment and we keep the Cad one more day. We'll leave it in a lot somewhere and tear up the ticket. Maybe in Corpus Christi. We buy a heap and head east. Once we both get clear, we can talk about where and when we split up."

"But first we got to get across the bridge into Brownsville," she said dully.

He drove the hard heel of his hand against the side of her head. She nearly fell. "What was that for?" she demanded angrily. "That hurt!"

"The next time you talk like the roof was falling in, you get it again."

"And nobody pushes me around, Benson."

He hit her again, harder than before. He said, "O.K., make a stink. Go complain to people. Go ahead."

She cursed him. He hitched up his pants and took a quick step toward her, and she could see, in the car lights, the faint gleam of his grin, the narrowness of his eyes. She backed away quickly. "No, don't! Don't do it again!"

"Say you're sorry."

"I'm sorry, Del."

"From now on you do everything I tell you to do, and you do it exactly the way I want it done." He reached out and his hand closed on her breast.

"Don't Del. My God!"

"We got to keep straight."

"Let go of me. You'll give me a cancer. You're crazy or something. Ow!"

"We get it understood right now."

She started to cry, helplessly, hopelessly. He released her. She backed away, leaned against a tree. He had turned away from her with sudden indifference. She continued to weep, silently. In a matter of a few moments, he had broken into a secret, independent part of her, and taken away something that had been hers. That hard core of independence. Men had tried to tie her to them with gifts, with persuasion, with protestations of love. Pain had worked where other methods had failed. Pain and humiliation. She felt as though she had become property, had become owned by this cocky little heavy-shouldered man with the face that looked as though you couldn't hurt it with a hammer. She knew that she would go with him, and that he would hurt her again, out of irritation, or anger, or indifference, or just to amuse himself. And she would take it, and stay around for more. She wept for herself, and for the lost years.

He's quick and he's as strong as a little bull, and somehow he's got me. There's something crazy in him, something all twisted, and it must be the same with me or I'd walk out right now when there's time. Walk out, or else ride with him to the bridge and say to the American customs, "This man here is wanted for murder in Mexico." Let them take him, and even tell them he shot Darby. God, how that hurt! It's going to hurt for days. I can tell by the way it feels now. Pain so I wanted to faint, and yet with it all screwed up somehow in my mind so that even while he was doing it, it made me start to want him the way it happened over there on the other side of the road in that field. It's like I don't own myself any more. Like he put a brand on me.

It's like with Big Mary, and that little twerp guy of hers that used to come up and beat on her and she took it. She cursed him every minute, but he didn't show up for a week and she'd start fretting about him, and she gave him every dime she could get together.

I don't want to be like that, but he's the same kind as Big Mary's guy. I can see that now. Someplace inside him he hates women. He uses them and hates them, maybe because he has to use them.

What's happened to me? This noon we were driving along the road, and I was thinking about all the things I bought, going over them all in my mind. And because a stinking little ferry keeps getting stuck in the mud, Darby is dead. He didn't call for help because he wanted to die. I know that. He waited for it. Darby's dead and I'm with this crazy little guy and I'll never be free of him again, never as long as I live. I want him, and I want him now. Here. And that's filthy, with Darby back there where we took him. That singing is driving me nuts. We've got to get across the river. We've got to run, run. I'll do what he says. He knows what he's doing. He's been in trouble before. God, what is happening to me?

Chapter Thirteen

JOHN CARTER GERROLD, stunned by the death of his mother, walked with long strides down the road, walked back toward the river. Without glasses, his eyes saw all the night lights haloed by astigmatic mist. He felt drained, exhausted.

If they hadn't finally brought the man around, that man who used to live in Kerrville, he never would have understood what they were trying to tell him.

Mamma would be kept there in San Fernando, and he had the undertaker's card, and he would have to go to Brownsville and make the necessary arrangements with a Brownsville undertaker to send for the body and fix up her papers at the border. Mamma had always liked things done efficiently and just so, and this sort of thing would have driven her crazy.

And the man who had lived in Kerrville had told him, in all seriousness, that in Mexico one could not transport a body past any cemetery without stopping and giving a sum of money to that cemetery. It was the custom. Who is to say, Señor, how much sense it makes? It is just a thing that is done here, and one cannot escape it. But as there are but three cemeteries between this place and the border, it does not make it expensive.

And then he had gone back to take another look at Mamma only to find, to his horror, that the man who had been ordered not to touch her had carefully applied a heavy coating of white face powder, plus rouge and lipstick and eye shadow. It made Mamma look as though she were the dead madam of a whore house. It took away every bit of her dignity. And in the end he had to pay twenty pesos for the labor of applying the make-up, and twenty more pesos to have it cleaned off.

He would think that he was over all the crying, and then a harsh sob would come out of his throat and it would start again. Mamma, painted up like a clown, had brought him right to the threshold of hysteria. That stupid grinning doctor had tried to make him take a powder, but he wasn't going to take anything when he didn't know what on earth it was. They could drug you and take all your money, and take Mamma's rings out of your pocket.

It was Linda who had insisted on this crazy Mexican trip, and it was the trip that had killed Mamma. Mamma had offered that perfectly good camp on the lake, just outside the Rochester city limits. It was familiar and pleasant. He had learned to swim out in front of the camp. The old desk upstairs was still cluttered with the things he had as a kid, the things that Mamma had said she'd save for her grandchildren.

She'd never see a grandchild. And if Linda got pregnant because of what they did while Mamma was dying, he hoped the baby would be born dead. And she could die having it. It would be justice, certainly.

Linda and all her cute ways. Mamma was right, way back in the beginning.

"Now, John, I know how taken you are with this . . . girl. She's as pretty as a picture. But, darling, you know she's been working in New York as a model, and those girls are not always . . . too virtuous. You can talk freely to Mother, dear. I'm not a Mid-Victorian type and you know it. Have you had intercourse with this girl?"

He remembered how shocked and angry he had been.

"Now, John, listen to Mother, and don't get so upset. I have the feeling that this is just an infatuation. You know it would be a very *good* marriage for her. She won't sleep with you because she is clever enough to know that if she did, then you might back out of this marriage."

"Mother, please! You're making it sound so . . . devious and dirty."

"I'm not implying anything of the sort. I just want to make absolutely certain that my boy isn't being too impulsive about this pretty little model."

"I'm going to marry her, no matter what you say or what you do."

Mamma had been right. So terribly right about the whole thing. And Linda had fooled him, right along. Laughed at him behind his back. That wedding-night business had obviously been just so much acting. Because certainly no virgin was suddenly going to begin acting the way she did in bed. It was easy to see that little Linda had been having herself a time, probably for years. All that funny talk about nothing being wrong when you were truly in love was just a feeble excuse for dirtiness. She was sex-crazy and Mamma had seen it and tried to tell him, and he had been too stubborn and too blind to see that Mamma was right, as usual. Linda had got what she wanted, a marriage that gave her the social position she didn't have. And if Mamma hadn't died like this, she might have got away with it. But now it was easy to see things clearly. She killed Mamma just as though she'd used a knife. She hated Mamma. You could see that the way she was trying to get him to go see his father. She wanted to go out there because she must have guessed that the woman Dad ran off with would be a kindred spirit. She and Linda would do well together.

I'm not going to let her get away with it, he thought. After this, I can't live with her. I couldn't touch her.

Mamma was clean and good and decent. That's why Linda couldn't stand her. She tried to hide it, but I could see it. Trying to make me think that Mamma hadn't done the right things, raising me the way she did.

I thought it was a face like an angel would have. Someday I'll be able to forget the filth and the craziness, but I'll never forget this day. Mamma was brave. She was accepting the marriage and trying to make me happy. She told us all about the little house she had looked at, just two blocks from our house. And Linda had been so funny and cold about it. No capacity for gratitude.

As far as I'm concerned, she can stay right here. She seems to love Mexico so much. Dotty Kale came here for her divorce. I won't marry again. I'll keep the big house just as it was. It will be a memorial for Mamma. There'll be all the books and the records and the garden. Somebody could come in to help share the expense. Maybe

Tommy Gill could give up his apartment and move in. We've always had such fun. And he's so clean-looking.

It will be good to be rid of her. Odd, how she is. When you see her standing at a distance, in the daylight, she has the clean dry look of an etching. But oh, in the tumbly night she's a dark and fleshy thing. The waist that looks by daylight as though it could be spanned with my two hands turns to a massive warmth. Buttocks and breasts swell overpoweringly thick and soft, heated and smothering, and she's at me like some animal, and there is no more cleanness in her, no crispness, no dryness, and while the cloying feeling of disgust at the vast softness of her sickens my mind, my animal body works at her, like some blind thing, until dirtiness is exploded within her and nothing is left but the sticky disgust, the unbearable desire to get away from her, but that's when she wants to be held, and wants to hear the tender words that can be parroted, even while they're acid in my mouth.

The statue was cold and clean in the midnight garden moonlight, and the cold breast was hard and good against my cheek, the loins like ivory.

He squinted across the river and saw that fewer cars than he expected had been brought across. The ferry was on his side and the planks had just been put in place. He moved aside to let the cars go by.

He went up one of the planks on the ferry deck and moved to the front of the craft. The lead cars in line had their lights on, and the lights made silver of the muddy river. Cars came on behind him and he didn't turn. He watched the far bank come steadily closer. The time to say it was now. Take her aside, in the darkness, and tell her she was filth, that she was a murderess, that she was dirty-minded. Say it coldly, as Mamma would say it. And then it would be all over, and there would be no more pretending.

She had been a temporary insanity. A craziness that had cost Mamma her life. He remembered striking her. Remembered it with satisfaction. She had been laughing inside herself, thinking of how she had won over Mamma. He'd broken the lying mouth on her, shaming her prop-

erly in front of the others, who weren't properly aware
of the way she was gloating.

He stood straight, weak eyes searching the night shore
for the pallor of her hair, the slightly darker texture of
the tan linen dress. He thought he could make out the
Buick back in the line, but he could see no one near it and
the lights were off. As soon as the first plank was in place,
unblocked, he walked down it, ignoring the incomprehensible complaints of the workmen. The first four cars were
gone, and that would mean the man named Danton was
gone, in his pickup truck. He was glad Danton was gone.
The gun-bearing guards had dealt almost contemptuously
with him, but Danton had given them trouble, had raised
his voice boldly to the fat toad in the lead car.

John walked up the road to the Buick and looked inside. She wasn't there. The two cars came off the ferry and
the two lead cars took their places aboard. He felt for
the keys and they were not there. Motors were starting
up and down the line, ready to move forward to the vacated places. John got in the car and got behind the wheel.
Linda would see the cars move and she'd be along with
the keys, and maybe this was the place to do it. Though
the windows had been down, there was a faint odor of
sickness in the car. The sun heat had left the metal, so
that it was just enough less than body temperature to feel
faintly cool to his touch.

And, in the unmoving air within the car, he could
detect Linda's perfume. In the beginning it had pleased
him. A light, flowery fragrance. But he had learned to
detect the rotten ripeness beneath the fragrance.

He heard her then, heard her light fond laugh, and it
was like a blow across his heart. How could she laugh?
A man laughed with her, his voice deep and slow, and
then, incredible thing, they sang together. "And I'll be in
Scotland afore ye. But me and my true love . . ."

The sick anger propelled him out of the car. He
whirled, facing them, slamming the car door hard behind
him, ending their song with its explosive note.

"Are you happy, Linda?" he shouted, his voice rising
thin and high. "Are you real happy, darling?"

"John, what are you doing here?"

"What are you doing? That's a better question. Who is that with you? Danton? Isn't she fun, Danton? Isn't she a dream?"

"Easy, boy, easy," Danton said in his low, slow voice.

"That's a good word for her too. Easy."

"John! Lower your voice."

"No, I'd rather sing to show you how happy I am. Sing with me, Linda. Come on, now. Are there any words to the Funeral March?"

"John, I know you're upset, but don't make a scene."

"I couldn't take her to Brownsville tonight. The undertaker in Brownsville will have to arrange to have her brought across the border. What do you care whether I make a scene? You obviously don't give a damn one way or the other. You couldn't stand being without a man for a few hours."

Linda started to cry. John watched her, feeling a good satisfaction. Tears like that were obviously faked.

"Give her a break, Gerrold," Danton said. "She was pretty blue. I was trying to cheer her up a bit."

"Obviously."

"You left her to drive the car to Matamoros. That's no job for a girl. I didn't think she could get it up those planks."

"She's an expert driver, Danton. You're just gullible. Why don't you leave us alone? This is a husband-and-wife quarrel. You're not wanted."

"Guess I'll just sort of listen in, if it's O.K. with Linda."

"Then listen and be damned to you. Linda, you can stop pretending to cry now. You haven't got enough heart to be the crying type."

"Please, oh, please," she said.

"You just happened to get caught sooner than you expected. If we stayed together I'd have caught you at it sooner or later. You know that as well as I do."

He saw her head lift. He could see her shadowed eyes. A car behind the Buick honked impatiently. John Gerrold ignored it.

"What are you trying to say?" she asked.

"I'm through. I don't care where you go or what you do after this." His voice broke on the last words. He took a deep breath. "You can get a divorce any way you want it. If there's a child, you can have it and I'll contribute to its support. But I don't want you around me. Mamma had to die to open my eyes to how cheap and common you are. I think she'd be glad to know I'm doing this. You can keep the things I've given you, and I'll finance the divorce."

She rubbed at tears with the back of her hand, with two quick gestures. "Are you quite certain you know what you're saying, John? When did you decide that? After you saw me with Mr. Danton?"

"Don't flatter yourself that much, my dear. I decided it on the other side of the river. I was going to break it to you a bit more easily, that's all. You two gave me the excuse to be blunt. I'm thankful for that. It saves time. Well, Linda?"

Astonishingly, Danton chuckled.

"This amuses you, Danton?"

"In a way, I guess you could say it does."

"You have a funny sense of humor."

"Oh, he has!" Linda said. "He's a perfect riot. He'll have you rolling on the ground."

The car honked again. John got in and moved the Buick down. He got out of the car again. Danton said, "You need any help with the arrangements you have to make?"

"I can manage."

"You'll have to take Mr. Danton to Matamoros, John. His friend is waiting for him there."

"I'll take both of you there. It doesn't matter one way or the other."

He decided that he had hit exactly the right note of indifference. They didn't seem to be as uneasy as he would have liked.

She said softly, "It will seem odd to get a divorce when all the time you weren't married to me. You were married to your mother."

"She knew what you were the moment she saw you.

She told me and I wouldn't believe her. She said you—"

"Better take it a little easy, Gerrold," Danton said in his soft way.

"So it's all right if the nastiness comes out of her mouth. It's all right if she says lewd things. But when I—"

"You gave up your claim, Gerrold. I'm staking one."

"Didn't take long, I see," John said. "How many before me and how many after you, Danton? She's a—"

"You keep talking and you're going to say something you'll wish you'd never thought of."

"Both of you, stop it," Linda said. "I won't be squabbled over like—like some sort of floozy. I'll get the divorce, John, if that's what you want. Yesterday it would have mattered a great deal. Today it doesn't seem important. I'm past feeling anything, one way or the other."

"Little walk won't hurt you, Linda. Little airing."

John watched them walk away, silhouetted against the car lights, and his wife was small beside the tall Danton. It gave him, for just a moment, a curious sense of loss. He tried to shrug it off.

He got back into the car and folded his arms across the top of the steering wheel, rested his forehead on his arms. "I did what you'd want me to do," he said. And he waited a moment and the tears came. "All alone," he said, and the tears came faster, channeling beside his nose, wet-salting his lips.

Such a damnable waste. Mamma was in her prime, really. Everybody respected her. We were such good pals. Just last year, coming home from school for vacation, and then having dinner, and Pauline in the kitchen clearing up afterward, and the way Mamma would give me that sly look across the room and without a word I'd set up the table and get the cards and the Russian-bank game would be on.

Or other nights, just listening to the records. Or reading to each other. If it wasn't for Linda it could still have been that way. And then coming into my bedroom, tucking me in as though I were a little kid.

She told me a lot of things. She never told me what a dirtiness marriage is. How it humiliates your body.

I can go back there alone and I can make myself well and whole again. I've got to get over Linda the way you get over an illness. And the house will be so desperately empty. There's no good reason for Tommy to keep that sleazy little apartment. I can make it very inexpensive for him. That school certainly can't pay him very well.

Tommy will know what I mean. He's the one I'll tell it all to. Every bit of it. I guess he still thinks of that time two years ago when we were both counselors at Camp Raedor, and that moonlight walk we took, when the whole world was an impossible silver, touching every leaf, and the beauty was so great it filled up your throat, and how it seemed so natural for us to walk hand in hand that night. Back in the lights it seemed odd to us that we'd done that, but it was right while we were in the moonlight. Tommy said then that true friendship can exist only between two men, and that women do not know the meaning of the word. He explained how a woman's existence is so functional a thing, and tied in so grimly with the business of procreation, that there is no room in their souls for friendship as such. I argued the point with him, but now I know he was right. And Mamma was right. And I was blind and wrong. I'll forget all those little scenes between Linda and me. Some of them will be hard to forget. They left deep scars.

His chin touched the horn ring and the horn blatted, shocking him with the noise. He slouched in the seat, resting his head on the back of the seat. The day had bitten deeply into his reserves of strength. There was a dull ache at the place where he had been struck by the gun barrel.

If he could take just a short nap, between ferry trips, it would help a lot. Mamma always said the way to relax and go to sleep quickly is to think of something beautiful.

He thought of a moonlit garden at night, and a statue gleaming white in the moonlight. He could see it from the porch door of his uncle's house. And he walked out, the dew cold against his bare feet.

There in the car, with his eyes closed, he could see the statue across the years. He moved closer to it. Now he was actually in the garden. He walked up to it, and it seemed as though he had never really looked at it before. Uncle was silly, calling it Diana, and calling it a girl. Anybody could see it was the marble statue of a young, clean-limbed boy. Flat white symmetry of chest, and the careful interweaving of the muscles of the flanks. He stood in the dream garden and the statue turned, bright and shocking and beautiful in its nakedness, pure in its perfect maleness. It stepped down from the pedestal and it held out its hand and he saw at once that it was Tommy, as he had known it would be. And he touched the firm cool hand, and Tommy spoke, calling him Linda. He tried to pull his hand away, protesting, but Tommy held it tightly, and he was Linda and John all at once, and he tilted his face upward . . .

"Sorry, Gerrold," Danton said, joggling his elbow. "We'll be second car on this load."

John struggled up out of sleep, and the knowledge that Mamma was dead fell in on him, like the crashing of a tall white room. He sobbed aloud.

"Move over, boy," Danton said gently. "I'll run it aboard."

Chapter Fourteen

Phil Decker walked up the road, through the night, away from the river, away from the cars, lifting his knees high with each stride, swinging his arms briskly. He walked away from the singing of the twins until there was no sound in all the world but the clip-tamp of his steps, the brush of fabric as the legs of the maroon shorts rubbed together.

No need to get excited about it. World's full of them. Kids with stars in their eyes and a little talent and a lot of ambition. God, if all the young babes with a yen for show business were laid end to end—it would probably get them someplace. Whose joke was that? Manny's? Sounded like him.

No need to think it was the end of the world. There were a lot of creeks and he'd been up most of them, spoonless as usual, and landed on his feet. But it was the interruption that mattered this time. Damn it, a man gets old. How long to pick up more partners and shape them up for the assault on TV? Two years? Not much less, certainly. They say, "Where have you played?" and you got to have an answer. And by that time he'd be over fifty.

The twins were soft in the head. What could they do all alone? Go back to that corn-fed routine they were doing first time they were booked? Or maybe go into one of those showcase jobs? That isn't an act. It isn't talent. Just walk around slow in a thousand bucks' worth of costume, giving the ringside baldies a glassy smile, and wagging those things God gave you, in a genteel way, and praying that one of the baldies wants to get closer than ringside, and the price for that is marriage. And backstage those big lovelies pop on the shell-rimmed glasses and read Proust or something, so that maybe if the baldie they get ever wants to talk, they can Proust the hell out of him.

It isn't an act, damn it. Now that strip, that's it. The only twin strip act on the road. The others can do it under water, or with birds, or with a tambourine, but I got the only strip twins in the business. I mean I had the only twins.

Talk them out of this craziness. The heat did it. The heat and this waiting. But I know them too well. They're sort of bright, and they're both stubborn. Hard as hell to make them change their minds. And this time they're like iron. You can feel it.

Every time the breaks come along, the timing is bad. Hell, a few years back we could have booked on that Keith merry-go-round and made a million bucks and they wouldn't have been unhappy.

Maybe they just can't take that strip. They seemed to be getting used to it. That can't be it. Just like old Billy Moscow. Remember how he picked up that lassy in Trenton? Dear Lord, how she was stacked! Ten days we spent, the two of us, trying to get her to do a strip. No, sir. Not that girl. Undress in front of *people?* she kept saying. And then a year later old Billy goes to Miami and what does he see but the same girl, calling herself Dixie Ravel, and not only is she doing a strip, but one with tassels that she gets spinning in opposite directions. A real talent. Billy was fit to be throat-cut over that.

I didn't ask for no bumps and grinds out of those girls. That's cheap stuff. Just a good dignified strip, and who the hell is going to fit into all those terrific expensive costumes now?

This next couple of years was going to be the good old days, for sure. Figured I had them coming to me. Thirty-three years of learning the timing. Thirty-three years. Gets so you can't remember what happened where. Twenty years with Manny. Decker and Malone. Songs and frolic. Top billing at the Orpheum three times. Paid one little girl fifty bucks a week and all she ever had to do was walk across the stage twice. That was with the gag where Manny follows her lugging that forty pounds of ice in a pair of tongs and then come weaving back out with one little bitty ice cube in those tongs.

A lot of years and a lot of happening. Never forget the yell that went up that night in Kansas City. We were to come on next. That was when that Austrian was acting funny. He had good reason to. One of the acrobats had been getting to his wife and the Austrian had a good hunch. So with her out there against the board he throws the knives fine, and he throws two of the hatchets fine, and with that last hatchet he cuts her in half, right from the eyebrows up. Got away with it, too. Told the cops the night was so hot his hand got sweaty. Sobbing and carrying on. We all knew the score, but nobody would snitch to local cops. That acrobat was pretty irritated, and he got even in a way only an acrobat could think up. He waits until the Austrian gets himself another wife and target, and then he gets to her too. Last I heard, the Austrian cut his throat with one of his own knives.

Sixteen that year I started. A singer, yet. Serious about it. Trying too hard. Then with the rose-colored spot on me, and singing something about somebody's mother, I swung my arm and knocked the prop loose on the baby grand and it came down and damn near broke my wrist. My God, the yuk that went up! Did something to me. So we put it in the act, and from then on I'm a comic. Had a big leather thing under my sleeve so that lid could come down with a real bang.

Billed with the best. Cantor and Berle's mother. Mickey Rooney when he was a three-year-old squirt stealing the stage from his whole damn family. All the vaudeville, and then the burlesque years, and then, with Manny gone, doing the singles in clubs.

Bert Lahr and that damn n-guh, n-guh, n-guh noise of his. All he had was the right break. Like Ed Wynn. And Joe Brown. Hell, I'm only forty-nine. That Lahr is right up there and he must be older than God. There's a lot of years left. Manny and I, and that thousand a week for damn near eight years. Half a million bucks and where did it go? We lived good because it was going to last forever, and Manny kept needling me for saving up dough and he was right, because as soon as I had fifty thousand bucks that bitch Christine busts in on me with two wit-

nesses when I'm with that little girl—can't even remember
her name or how it was. I hope it was good, because the
settlement on Christine was fifty thousand bucks, a con-
siderable amount to pay for one little tumble. Manny
laughed so hard he couldn't hardly stand up and he told
me that's what I get for saving money.

It was going to last forever and somehow it didn't. I
got my health and the car and fifteen hundred bucks and
a load of costumes. No time to give up, Phil boy. But
you can wonder about that health angle. I know I ought
to see a doc. The way my left arm keeps going numb
every once in a while, and when it's numb, I can't seem to
get enough air in my lungs when I take a breath. Hell,
that isn't enough of a symptom to bother a doc with. No
pain. I'm as tough as I ever was.

Say, I must have walked a mile and a half. Stop and
take a breather. Lot of stars in the sky. Makes you feel
tiny, like you're on stage in the biggest damn theatre
in the world. Stars always make me think of backdrops,
of the ceiling of clubs. Funny how all the time they
want to go making decorations that look like stars.

Make jokes out here and you don't get much of a
laugh, that's for sure.

Why did they have to do it to me?

Well, I let them know I can get along fine without
them. Fine and dandy. Hard to find twins for an act,
though.

Doesn't pay to be alone. Makes you gloomy. Making
me wonder just what in the hell I'll do if I can't whump
up another act. Nobody to go to. No trade but the one I
got. Some tired costumes and a car that needs a motor
overhaul, and a headful of jokes and lyrics. A million of
them. Name any object and I can give you three gags on
it, clean or blue. Fountain pen, post office, mallard duck.
Any object. Can't remember where the gag came from.
Got a hundred ways to squelch hecklers. Please, mister, do
I come over to where you work and keep joggling your
shovel? Lady, please, we both got professions. Yours is
just a little older than mine.

I'll kill 'em in the old men's home. They'll rock and

cackle, rock and cackle, all day long. That Decker feller, he's sure a card.

I've slept in ten thousand beds, drunk a thousand barrels of liquor, bounced more hundreds of women than I want to think about. I've made a half million bucks and spent all of it but fifteen hundred. I've never cheated a friend, or chiseled a buck, or kicked over a baby carriage. Why do I stand here hitching? Just because a pair of stacked blondes double-crossed me. Couple of years from now I won't even remember their names or what they look like. Couple of years from now they'll see this ugly puss on magazine covers and know they pulled the craziest stunt in the world. My pattern can't miss. It can't miss. It's what people want. A little music, a little skin, a touch of the blue. They want visual gags, and that's perfect for TV. Maybe I can get a single on TV. Wouldn't take much practice to work up that thing I used to do years ago. Leon Errol, God rest his soul, used to do it better. Old rubber legs.

Let me see, I'm carrying the glass like this, and I do the rubber-leg deal, coming on, drinking what's in the glass and leaving that big chunk of glass that looks like ice. I get the hiccups. I get them so bad, like this, while I'm staggering around, that the ice goes way up in the air, and each time I get the glass in the way and it falls back in. Then comes a big hiccup and the ice goes up and I turn around and it drops right into that gap at the back of my pants. Now let's see. . . .

There in the starlight, in the middle of the empty road, in the middle of the empty burned land, the little man staggered and weaved and hiccuped, holding an imaginary glass. After a big hiccup he stood very still, his face showing wonderment. He looked into the glass, then looked around the TV stage. No ice. Wonderment turned slowly to shock, and then to consternation. He did a wild, gesticulating dance, and quite suddenly stopped.

He shook his left arm as though trying to flip water from the fingertips. He massaged his left hand hard, breathing deeply. He rubbed his arm for a time and then turned toward the river and walked back.

He walked lifting his knees high and swinging his arms briskly, and in the night was the clip-tamp of his steps and the faint rasp of fabric, and the long, long rain sound of that kind of applause that stops the show, every time.

Chapter Fifteen

LINDA walked beside Bill Danton, grateful for his silence, grateful for the understanding that caused his silence. A faint night breeze was cool on her shoulders.

"What do they call it?" she said at last. "A swing and a miss, I guess. That's the way I feel."

"Get yourself all readied up to make a big decision, and he makes it for you."

"I ought to feel relieved. I just feel empty."

"He was rough."

"He's not the same John. Not the same as yesterday."

"Linda, he hated you yesterday, and shows it today."

"But he didn't, really. I know he didn't."

"O.K., then it was like something balanced in his mind. A big round boulder on the top of a hill. It was going to roll down one side or the other."

"That makes more sense. I can understand that better, Bill. But what's going to become of him? He needs me."

"Give him a few years if you want to throw yourself away. Anyhow, I don't think you could if you wanted to. That boy is done. He's through."

"And here we are?"

"That's what I'm trying to tell you, Linda."

She stopped and faced him, looking up at him, the hair paler in the starlight than the honeyed tan of her face.

"Bill, I'm not a great brain. I haven't been alive long enough to learn much. But there's a funny kind of knowledge in me. I don't like pat answers. I don't like neat, hemstitched little endings on my stories. Life doesn't come out that way. There's never exactly the right amount of string to tie up a package. Always too much or too little. Pat endings are from O. Henry and Metro-Goldwyn-Mayer and Edgar Guest. I can't have my marriage blow up in my face and give a big contented sigh and fall into your arms and we walk away into the sunset

160

with violin music. No, Bill. Life doesn't work that way."

"I can see what you're trying to say. But maybe this time it does work that way. Maybe this is the one time when there's just enough string for one package."

"I don't want a rebound job. Neither do you. You'd be a wonderful shoulder to cry on. A nice big wall for my tears. But I can't see myself doing it. No doubt you're a sweet guy, a find, something every girl should have. But I'm a girl with a lot of cat in me. Ever see a hurt cat, Bill?"

"Can't say as I have."

"They go away. They go off by themselves, Bill, and they tend to themselves and the hurt gets better or it kills them. So I'm not going to fall in your arms, though God knows I want to. I don't want to be alone. I wasn't made to be alone. I was made for one man. John doesn't seem to be the one. Maybe you aren't, either. I'm in no condition to even guess about you."

"Let me do all the guessing."

"No. Write out your address and give it to me. I'm going to get a Nevada divorce. And when it's final, I'm going back to New York and use what contacts I still have to get back into modeling work. And once I'm all set, Bill, if I'm still thinking about you and still wondering, I'll write and you come up to my environment where I can get a look at you. I can't see anything clearly here in Mexico. Then there won't be any question of a rebound. And there won't be any strings on me, and maybe I'll have stopped feeling so empty."

She looked at him, waiting for his comment, knowing that this would, in a sense, be a measure of his maturity. If he knicked up a fuss, argued with her, criticized her plan, it could mean that he lacked a certain necessary quality of assurance. She wanted no more uncertain men in her life. The relationship with John had been odd and wrong. He had made all the little decisions. What dress she would wear, where and when they would eat. And yet, with the chips down, as in the matter of where to go for the honeymoon, she had made the decision. She wanted a man this time. She wanted to be able to wheedle and get her way in little things, and have him decide big things.

He scuffed the sole of his sandal on the hard surface of the road. "Sure like to kidnap you and take you home and show you off and say, 'See why I waited and see what I found.' But I see what you mean. It would be moving too fast. Got to sweat it out a little. Got to work and pray for it a little. But one thing, Linda. You're it. For me. Sure, it's only one day, and not even a whole day at that. So what do I know, or maybe it's better to say *how* do I know? Because you lived a long day. You've been through a lot. With me watching. More than if I'd known you for months and months when nothing was happening."

"You can't be sure so quickly, Bill."

"Doesn't make much sense, does it? Man goes around trying to make sense of what happens in his heart, he has a pretty hard time, I guess. I'm no kid. All I can say is this: Somewhere in the back of my mind I've been building me a woman. Doing it for years. Everybody does, I guess. Then you come along and I get what those art critics call 'the shock of recognition.' You're like you walked out of my own head, like I built you myself.

"I don't expect you to have that same shock of recognition. I just want to be liked. And I'd be low-rating myself if I didn't believe that liking is going to turn to love, if I work at it. I like to hoot and holler and stomp around. I need an earthy woman and a laughing woman and a loving woman. Pretty comes next, and you got that market pretty near cornered, and that's like pure profit."

"I'm not all those things."

"Maybe not. But you'll be them to me, and that's where it counts. So I respectfully submit that your planning needs one other little thing."

"Like what?"

"Like writing me your address as soon as you're divorced and in New York. I won't come roaring right up. I'll give you time. But I want the chance to sell you a bill of goods, whether you want to listen to the salesman or not. And then I won't feel as if you were gone."

"O.K., Bill. That's fair. What if I said I wouldn't give it to you?"

He laughed softly. "I've got the license number of the Buick written down. Don't imagine it would be much of a trick to trace you through Gerrold."

"Just for that I ought to make you do it."

"Had to use the pencil that Atahualpa gave me. Only thing I could think of at the moment."

"Bill, we won't be able to say good-by in Matamoros. We kissed and I said a silly thing, and it leaves a bad taste. Could another one be sort of arranged?"

"You're putting me to a lot of trouble, but perhaps . . ."

"I want the kind of kiss that's for luck. A friendly kiss."

He pulled her over to where the shadows were deep, pulling her lightly by the wrist. She felt his big hands on her shoulders, saw the dark loom of his face over hers, tilted her face up to his. His lips were firm on hers, firm and warm. A short kiss and one that was very sweet. He still held her shoulders and then his fingers bit deep and his lips came down again as he made a small sound in his throat, half groan and half sob. She fought herself for one twisting moment and then returned his kiss with a crazy, unexpected kind of hunger. They parted and she stood, strangely dazed.

"Good-by, Linda," he said.

"Good-by . . . Bill Danton."

"Looks like we'll get across this trip."

"You go to the car. I'll be along in a minute."

"Sure."

He disappeared, heading toward the car. She touched her fingertips to her lips. The kiss had shaken her more than she had let him know. A funny thing for a kiss, she thought, in this day and age. A kiss was something bestowed on a casual acquaintance without thought of implication or complication. Yet her response had been almost instantaneous. She had responded to his maleness, to the rude force of him, so gladly and so thoroughly that even now, minutes later, her breasts still tingled, her knees were not yet strong. John had never done that to her with a kiss, nor had anyone else.

She thought, Am I being a stupid girl, responding to high square shoulders and a Texas drawl? Or just a bitch, made ready and willing in the space of one breath? Or is it this crazy day, working on me like an aphrodisiac, day heavy with death, eaten with tensions—cancerous, ulcerous day?

No, behind the façade of the unlettered drawl and the torn T shirt there's a sensitive, educated, understanding guy. I responded to that, plus the maleness. And I responded because I had no fear.

She walked slowly to the car. Bill was behind the wheel, easing the Buick down to the car ahead. John had slid over onto the passenger side of the front seat. She opened the door and got into the back.

Bill said, "Driven this road a hundred times, Gerrold. Glad to drive if you want me to."

"Go ahead. It doesn't matter."

She could tell by the fusty sound of his voice that he had napped. He always seemed cross and dull when he awakened, as though sleep took him to a place where he spent his dreams on a witness stand, lying to tireless examiners. She thought she had known him, and yet she had not. She had often watched him sleep, looking at him as though to memorize every detail of him. A man of her own. And today she had found out that it was not a man at all, but rather a precocious, clever child, masquerading in a man's body—willful, petulant, and very bright.

She had given herself to the man body, tried to teach it a litany of ecstasies, only to find the inner child convulsed with shyness. Love had become a stilted dance with each step in proper order, leading, in the end, to the graceful formal bow and the end of the music.

And even as she sat there, in the space where her mother-in-law had been taken ill, she thought that deep within her, against the womb wall, an ovum might be beginning that miracle of cell division, progressing from formlessness, moving up the slow ladder of evolutionary stages, becoming at last a human being with 50 percent of its heredity coming from John Carter Gerrold.

She pressed her hand hard against the smooth swell of

her abdomen under the linen. Poor little beastie. But there would be enough love in the world so that it could have some. Love from her. Love from Bill.

She smiled wryly in the darkness. Her subconscious was taking off with seven-league boots. Marrying her up with Bill without the slightest qualm. Assuming his willingness to take on the responsibility of the child, and love it too, merely because it happened to be half hers.

In effect it was like having two husbands sitting side by side in the front seat of the car. Step right up and compare them, folks. Here we have Exhibit A. And this one is Exhibit B. Note the configuration of the skulls, the shape and placing of the features. One is a man and one is an imitation. Can you tell which one is Mr. Famous Man and which one is smiling, popular salesman Jack Peterson from the Bronx? If you guess correctly, we shall send you, without obligation, one slightly worn wife. A little gloss has been rubbed off the edges, and the item is slightly flawed by tear stains, but it is guaranteed to function with all the efficiency you have come to expect from any product of this reliable firm.

As the wheels reached the planks the front end of the car began to lift. She closed her eyes. Life had begun again. Life and movement. And she could sleep, knowing that somehow, someday, that movement would take her to a good place. A good place to be. When you stopped believing that, you stopped believing anything.

Epilogue

MANUEL FORNO, ferryman, could not remember ever having been so tired. He was so weary that it frightened him a bit. At noon, after hours of the senseless, infuriating shovel work in the muddy river, when he and the others had decided to quit until the beast of a river established itself at one level, the passengers on both sides of the river had made up a bonus of pesos and given it to the aged official in charge of the ferry.

Vascos, may his ears rot, had doled the pesos out with extreme cleverness. Had he given out too little, they would all have quit working anyway. Had he given out too much, the result would have been the same.

So it was body-racking work, hour after hour, with the pesos suspended just a little way in front of you, like a carrot suspended in front of a goat. What a vast feat of the intellect, to procure a ferry too large for the river it was to service! A typical maneuver of the bureaucrats in the capital city of the state. No, he would not work like a burro. Either the ferry goes, or Manuel Forno goes. Ah, the old ferry! The old scabby darling that would float in a single cup of water. This was indeed progress.

Every time he tried to stand still, his legs began to tremble. He felt as though his arms hung from red-hot wires laced through the flesh of his back and shoulders.

Never had there been, in all memory, such a day.

Why was it so essential in the vast scheme of the universe that so many vehicles should wish to cross the Río Conchos in one small day?

He was a brown, slant-shouldered man, taller and thinner than average. He had fierce brows, wicked-looking eyes. He was a very mild man.

The night was better than the sun, at least. Yet he could have wept of a broken heart when that monstrous fool from Victoria tumbled his truck into the waters, directly

166

in the way of the ferry. It meant ceaseless grubbing in the mud, bracing of jacks, planting of blocks, prying with timbers before the evil thing regained its feet and sat fat and gloating over the trouble it had caused.

Back in the wonderful days of the aged ferry, Manuel Forno had taken much pleasure in the work. It was amusing to inspect the tourists, pleasant to chat with familiar passengers from the nearby towns. And there were many hours when no traffic appeared and it was possible to do exactly nothing. The only flaw at that time had been the incredible stubbornness of all vehicles. If they were at the west bank of the river, invariably the first car to appear would be on the opposite shore. It was then possible to pretend to be blind and hope that one would appear on the west bank, but soon the car would grow impatient and begin to yelp loudly for attention.

On this day the only passenger he noticed with any interest was Atahualpa. Ah, how the shovels flew then! There were black stories of Atahualpa. Of his long memory, of persons punished and rewarded, without cause.

And who could say? One day he might control the state, and had he detected either laziness or insolence at the Río Conchos ferry, he might take it into his head to construct a bridge. But the danger was even more immediate. A shot had been fired. A tourist had been struck on the head. Evidently Atahualpa was impatient.

So Manuel had called on reserves of strength to hasten Atahualpa's crossing, conscious of the bleak, expressionless eyes perhaps focused on his naked back. A mere nod and a gesture and Rosalita might be caused to purchase many candles and pay for a mass.

So it was midnight, and but one car waited on the far bank. All the rest had gone. One last willful beast of a car, squatting there and demanding passage across the river. Manuel stopped to lift the heavy plank and found, to his dull amazement, that he could not straighten up with it. He walked out of the shallow water on legs that felt like stilts, and sat down the moment he was on dry land.

Vascos came bustling over. "So? So? A vacation, perhaps?"

"I cannot do more. I do not believe that I can walk home."

"Never in one day have you made more pesos, my friend. And this is your gratitude?"

"Nor have you made more, Vascos, and you have done no work. You have rushed about, flapping your arms like a chicken thinking of weasels."

"I will not stand for insolence, Manuel."

"Flap your arms more quickly. The breeze is refreshing."

"I command you to work."

"Vascos, truly, I cannot. It is impossible."

Vascos sighed. "Perhaps that is true. You have worked the hardest. Go home, then, Manuel. And tomorrow you will come to work at noon, perhaps?"

"Perhaps. If I do not die of sleeping too heavily."

He sat on the bank and watched the ferry move over after the last car. Unlighted trucks, too heavy for the planks, sat in the shadows and waited for tomorrow, when the steel ramp could be used.

Manuel looked at the stars for a time, gave an enormous sigh, and got to his feet. He lightly touched the pocket where he could feel the comforting wad of peso notes. A half of one month's pay for but one day's labor. Yet there was nothing unfair about it. On this beast of a day he had done the full labor of half a month. That incredible ferry goes, or Manuel Forno goes.

With his legs trembling under him, he trudged up the endless hill. A hundred yards from the crest of the hill he took a footpath that wandered vaguely off to the right. Insects whined in the night grass and his yawns were so violent that they squeezed his eyes shut and made him stagger. Ah, sleep! Endless, blessed, perfect sleep. His adobe hut with its grass roof was on a small plot of baked ground just over the crest of a small rise. As soon as he could see over the crest, he saw his house, casting its faint starlight shadow. He could see through the open doorway, see the pinkish glow of the charcoal fire atop the stone stove.

He walked loosely down the slope, letting his heels

strike with a force that jarred him. As he came close he
made out the plump, comfortable figure of Rosalita. He
looked down at her, smiling. She had fallen asleep waiting
for him, her back against the house wall, her forehead on
her knees.

He reached down and touched her shoulder gently. She
sprang awake.

"You are home!" she said.

"No, indeed, woman. I died of working like a burro. I
am a ghost visiting the scenes of a once happy life on
earth."

She stood up. "Do not joke of ghosts. And do not speak
so loudly, you will wake the children."

"All day, orders, orders. Manuel, do this. Manuel, do
that. Now carry the ferry across on your back, Manuel.
So here I am ordered about also."

"I went there twice. Both times that Vascos told me it
would be very late, and both times you were on the far
side of the river. Now you must eat."

"For that it will be necessary for you to grasp my chin
and make the motion of chewing for me."

"You cannot sleep empty."

"I can sleep empty. I can sleep on top of the fire. I can
sleep upside down with my toes fastened to the wall.
Woman, I shall give an exhibition of sleeping that will
become a part of recorded history."

"You must eat, Manuel," Rosalita said stubbornly.

She went into the house. He sat where she had been
sitting. Soon he heard a crackling, scented the odor that
drifted through the doorway. He struggled to his feet,
came out with an olla, poured cool water from it over his
head and shoulders. He smoothed his hair back with his
fingers. At times his legs would make uncontrollable
twitchings.

She brought out the food for him. Crisp tacos enfolding
the tender meat of young goat. He found that he could
chew and swallow, found that the food had in truth been
badly needed. And she had a special treat for him, a
bottle of dark beer that she had managed somehow to
keep cool. He knew of the bottle, and knew that she had

been saving it for a special occasion. So she gave it to him when he was weary.

He dug out the wad of pesos, deciding, after all, not to hide away a portion of them for any unexpected opportunity that might present itself.

"Is this . . . is this all pesos?"

"Ha! There are only five one-peso notes. The rest are five-peso notes."

"Who did you rob?"

"My old age. After today I shall die very young. Everyone will mourn. Vascos will weep bitterly. How can he obtain so stupid a burro elsewhere?"

"A dress for Conchita," she chanted. "And oil for the lamp and shoes for Ramón and the book to write in for Carlos."

"So, it is all gone?"

"Perhaps not. Perhaps you may have a centavo all to yourself."

"Once I was a happy unmarried man."

"Stop complaining. Tell me what happened during the day. Was there excitement?"

"Emilio, who drives the fish truck, became excited. Before he could cross the river all of the ice had melted away. Ah, the stench that began to rise! It affected even Emilio. As he drove off he was leaning forward as close to the front window as he could get, and he was breathing through his open mouth, with an expression of great pain."

"He will lose his position."

"Perhaps."

"A tragedy. What else?" she asked avidly.

"The great Atahualpa crossed our river. Such is his power that the trip was perhaps but fifteen minutes slower than on the other times he has crossed. I was disappointed. I wished him to snap his fingers so that I could see the waters part and he drive through to the other side."

"Do not speak sacrilege, please, Manuel. Anyway, I heard that he had crossed the river. Ana told me. What else happened?"

"What is the good of telling you if you know all before I open my mouth?"

"Perhaps I missed something," she said, giggling.

"One of Atahualpa's people fired a shot carelessly. Another one hit a *turista* on the head, sending him to sleep. The careless one was beaten and abandoned. One *turista* woman was sick, I believe, from the heat. The great Atahualpa brought her across the river. Let me see. One of Rodríguez' children was stung by a scorpion, but it was a small one. Much beer was drunk. Both store-keepers on the far side have made a fortune this day. Other than that, woman, there is nothing."

"Nothing? Were not the *turistas* angry?"

"Perhaps. Forgive me, but it is most difficult for me to think of them as people in the way that you and I are people. They seem more like those bright toys for children that we saw in Brownsville long ago. The expensive ones with the painted faces and the key in the back. Remember, the key is wound up and they dance or walk. It is that way with the *turistas*. They come to the bank of the river. The machine inside them stops. They wait. They cross the river. The machine starts up again and they go off at a furious pace. But people, no. Dolls of many bright colors."

"Ah, that is because you do not understand them. They have lives, too. A wait at the river, it could change many lives."

He snorted. "Woman, it made them late. So they drive madly half the night and catch up with the uninterrupted shadow of themselves and nothing is changed."

"Now perhaps I can tell you my news?"

"Again, woman! Again, so soon?"

"No. Apparently you think of but one subject."

"I am not aware of any new laws forbidding it."

"This is not that sort of news. Miguel Larra is dead."

It saddened him. "What sort of bull was it? One of Piedras Negras? They are killers."

"No, he was not fighting. He was killed by an American tourist. He was killed yesterday evening at his house in Cuernavaca. A girl was also killed. Larra's head was broken, but the girl was shot with a gun that shoots spears into fish."

"Is there such a gun?"

"That is what was said."

"Someone heard of this thing on a radio?"

"No."

"Saw it in a paper?"

"No."

"Woman, kindly do not attempt to infuriate me. I am far too weary for games. Perhaps a *zopilote* stopped and told you."

"No. It was María, she of the butcher."

"In a sense, I have always considered her a *zopilote*. But why do you drag it out in this manner? Like throwing crumbs to a chicken. How did María know? Tell me, woman."

"Today she was in Matamoros. She went with Fernando in the little truck. All Matamoros is talking about it. It is said that the murderer is fleeing for the border. There are many police. Every car leaving Mexico is being examined most carefully, and every *turista* is forced to answer many questions. They know the name of the man, but María could not remember it. She said it was a difficult name. And they have his description. It is said in Matamoros that even a mouse would find it difficult to creep out of Mexico. Perhaps the murderer was at the ferry. Perhaps you brought him across today."

"If you wish to dream, kindly go in and go to sleep. It is more fitting."

"Such a thing could happen!"

"No. It is of the class of things that might happen, yet never do. Perhaps he has been captured at Laredo already. In a week or two the government will permit the police of Matamoros to know that they can cease searching for the man. That is bad about Larra. And odd. Many have believed that a bull would get him. And so a *turista* kills him."

"Was there a nervous *turista* at the ferry?"

"How can I tell if one is nervous? To me, as I said, they are dolls with the key in the back. Now I must sleep or

die. Tomorrow you can make me deaf with talking.
Tonight, woman, I sleep."

They went inside to the pallets on which they slept,
side by side. Manuel squinted into the shadows, trying to
make out the sleeping forms of his four children. He
shrugged, peeled off his clothes, took the olla outside, and
did a bit more scrubbing, then dried himself and came to
bed. He was drunk with the idea of sleep. He sighed
heavily as he stretched out. He got into his favorite position, sighed again, and closed his eyes. They snapped
open as though there were little springs on the lids. He
shifted position, grunting, and tried again. Once again
the eyes popped open. One leg gave a convulsive twitch.
He carefully phrased a horrible curse and sat up.

"What is it, Manuel?" she whispered.

"All of my life I have done one thing well. I have slept.
There is no one in Mexico who is able to sleep any better
than Manuel Forno. People have walked miles to watch
how beautifully I sleep. And now, in the crisis of my life,
I have either forgotten how it is done, or something is
broken."

"Try again, my husband."

He tried again, sat up again. "It is no use. What am I
to do?"

She shifted toward him. "It is possible to get too tired
to sleep."

"Or too hungry to eat? That is nonsense."

"No, it is possible. I think there is a way one can sleep,
however. At least, it is evident that it is a way you have
fallen asleep more times than I care to count."

He reached for her. "What a fate to be chained to an
insatiable woman!"

"Remember, this is for your own good," she whispered,
giggling.

"To be taken as bitter medicine, then. I was far too
tired to walk home, so I am too tired for this. It will kill
me, certainly."

"A splendid death, *alma de mi vida.*"

His hands found the well-learned warmness, found her
body in the well-known way that soon made her breath

deep with a tiny audible catch in it. She sighed and they were joined, and in the hut was the tiny rustle of the pallet, their mingled breathings.

And afterward she held him, held his head against her breast, heard his breathing slow and soften into sleep. She held him and smiled into the night. He was a good man, and tender. He would never be much. Ambition was not in him, or any great imagination. But he was a husband to love dearly, because when he was in the house there was a warmth about it, a warmth and humor that departed when he went away. And that was a thing beyond price.

She thought of the ferry and then of the extra pesos, and then of the *turistas* and how this place had been merely an annoyance to them. A little place on a river, and yet it was her life, and Manuel's life and the lives of their children. They were always there, while the big cars whined through, carrying bright-faced people from incomprehensible places to unthinkable destinations. A little time by the river couldn't hurt them. A little time to breathe in the midst of journeying.

His sleeping weight had begun to make her uncomfortable. Gently she eased him away and into his proper place, cooing to him softly as to one of the children, covering him up against the night air.

A man to love and a place to sleep and now, for a time, a few extra pesos. It should be enough. Enough for gods.

All the weight of happiness seemed to come at once into her throat. She felt a quiver of superstition, that it was wrong to be this happy, that to be this happy courted misfortune. A car slipping on the ferry, crushing Manuel. The death of a child. An illness.

But to think of such things did not, somehow, diminish the extent of her happiness. They merely salted it a bit and made it more flavorful. Life moved too quickly. Rosalita wanted five hundred more years of exactly what she had.

ABOUT THE AUTHOR

John D. MacDonald was graduated from Syracuse University and received an MBA from the Harvard Business School. He and his wife, Dorothy, had one son and several grandchildren. Mr. MacDonald died in December 1986.